This book may be kept

FOURTEEN DAYS

A fine will be charged for each day the book
is kept over time.

Sep 24 '82	Oct 14 87		
Oct 18 '82			
Nov 15 '82			
Nov 29 '82			
Apr 8 83			
May 11 83			
Oct 31 83			
Nov 8 83			
Dec 31 83			
Feb 23 84			
Apr 30 84			
Aug 10 84			
Mar 14 85			
Jun 5 85			
Apr 29 86			
Oct 1 86			

ABIGAIL

ABIGAIL

a novel

Lois T. Henderson

CHRISTIAN HERALD BOOKS
Chappaqua, New York 10514

Christian Herald, independent, evangelical and interdenominational, is dedicated to publishing wholesome, inspirational and religious books for Christian families. "The books you can trust."

 MEMBER OF
EVANGELICAL CHRISTIAN
PUBLISHERS ASSOCIATION

Library of Congress Cataloging in Publication Data

Henderson, Lois T.
  Abigail: a novel.
  1. Abigail (Biblical character) — Fiction. I. Title.
PZ4.H51124Ab [PS3558.E486]   813'.54   80-65429
ISBN 0-915684-62-4

Third Printing
CHRISTIAN HERALD BOOKS, 40 Overlook Drive, Chappaqua, New York 10514
Printed in the United States of America

Dedicated to
our children,
David and Mary Ann
and
Mary Sue and Jim
With my love

preface

Although the Bible indicates that Abigail was beautiful and wise and perhaps even possessed a gift of prophecy, since it was she who foretold that David would rule Israel and establish an enduring house, there is nothing said about her son beyond the fact that he was born. To attempt to explain why he did not enter into the later conflict over who would succeed David, I have used a purely imaginary event which would have made him unfit to rule. As in all biblical fiction, such events are the product of the author's imagination, but I have striven always to adhere rigidly to the basic truths of the story as it is told in Scripture.

Once more, I want to express my deep gratitude to Gladys Donaldson for her suggestions and criticism and to Ruth Curry, who typed the manuscript. There are no adequate words to say how much I appreciate their help.

part I

Now there was a man in Maon...the man's name was Nabal, and his wife's name was Abigail.... And the woman was intelligent and beautiful in appearance, but the man was harsh and evil in his dealings, and he was a Calebite.

1 Samuel 25:2-3

1

THE HIGH WAVERING CRY of a lamb came from behind the tawny rocks that jutted their wind-carved, angular shapes against the blazing sky.

"How in the world did a lamb get down there?" Abigail asked anxiously.

Her brother, Benjamin, grinned. His breath was coming hard after his race into the town of Hebron and back to this grazing area. He had run home to tell Abigail she was needed in the fields. It had taken some skill to avoid their mother, but Zopporah was so caught up in her preparations for the coming feast that the roof could have fallen in and she wouldn't have noticed.

Or at least that was the hope that Abigail had expressed to Benjamin as she had hurried beside him back to the difficulty that only she could resolve.

"I tried to get the lamb out myself," Benjamin had explained. "But I'm too big to squeeze into the crevice, so Father told me to get you."

Now Abigail stood, surefooted, on a rocky ledge that dropped away toward the valley. A huge jumble of rocks formed sharp gullies and miniature mountains beneath the ledge. She repeated her question as she scrambled toward the narrow crevice. "How did a lamb get down there?"

"The silly ewe was trying to lead it up to the pasture and

let it get too close to the edge. I don't think it's really hurt — it doesn't sound like a hurt lamb — only scared. It's caught there, beyond the tall gray rock. You'll have to squeeze in between the ledge and the wall of stone."

"I know what to do," Abigail retorted. "I've done it often enough before."

The rough surface of the rocks scraped her arms and legs, and there was one terrifying moment when she felt she was going to plunge over the edge. But long practice helped her regain her balance and inch her way into the crevice that stretched to her right like a narrow, roofless cave.

As a quavering cry sounded almost at her feet, she looked down to see the small white lamb wedged between two stones. She was squeezed too tightly herself to bend down to pick up the frightened little animal, but she had encountered this difficulty before. Ignoring the jagged stone that bit into her flesh, she forced her elbows into niches in the rock so that her feet could swing free. Cautiously and slowly, she worked her slender bare feet around and under the woolly body. The lamb struggled frantically, making her lose her grip.

"Stupid thing!" she said. "Stand still!"

This time, she was able to pull the lamb free.

"Benjamin," she shouted, holding the lamb tightly with her feet. "Get down on your stomach and use your crook now. I've got the lamb freed."

Benjamin's first sweep with the staff caught Abigail's ankle, nearly causing her to lose her hold on the lamb.

"Be careful!" she yelled. "You'll make me drop it again."

This time the crook came more slowly and precisely than before. Using her feet, Abigail settled the lamb securely into the bend of the staff.

"Now," she shouted. "You've got it now. Pull very carefully. I'll push it along toward you. Gently — by all the gods, go gently!"

"Watch your tongue, girl! You know there are no gods but Yahweh. We don't use that expression in our family." Her father's voice came sharply. He must have come up to Benjamin after she had slid into the crevice.

Abigail grinned as she began the painful struggle back to where Benjamin and her father were waiting. She knew her choice of language often annoyed her father and shocked her mother. If Eliab were any other man, if he treated her as daughters were customarily treated, she would be whipped.

Of course, she reflected, nursing her scraped elbow and twisting lithely to get past the last rock, if she were treated like other daughters, she wouldn't be out here in the fields in the first place.

"Is the lamb all right?" she panted and then paused to suck furiously on her thumb where a graze had brought blood.

"The lamb is better off than you," Eliab said, looking at his daughter with dismay. "You really scraped yourself up good that time."

"Maybe she's getting too big for such rescues," Benjamin suggested and grinned. "After all, if she's old enough to get married, she's maybe too fat for such tight squeezes."

"I'm not one bit fatter than I was a year ago," Abigail shot back. "And besides, I'm not really old enough to get married. It's Father who thinks I am."

"Whether you think you're old enough or not isn't the important thing," Eliab said. "The man, Nabal, is rich and willing to wed you. If he thinks you're old enough, you're old enough."

Abigail looked up at her father. As tall as Benjamin was, Eliab stood taller still — his hair and beard as dark as his son's. "Benjamin's three years older than I am," Abigail said. "And he's not married yet."

"Never mind about Benjamin," Eliab replied. "When I find the right girl for him, he'll be married. Never fear."

Benjamin smiled at Abigail with wry sympathy. *It's a little like looking in a mirror to look at my brother,* Abigail thought. Their clear, dark eyes, their straight noses and full, curving mouths were almost identical. But that was as far as the similarity went. The boy was tall and sturdy, his hair a tumble of curls, while she was small and thin, her long, straight hair caught in a thick braid which hung down her back.

"It's not easy," Abigail muttered at last. "It's not easy to have to go to another village and marry a man who's more than twice as old as you are."

"But rich," Eliab said. "He'll be able to give you servants and gold bracelets and a fine house."

Abigail leaned down absently to pull a thorn from her foot. When she looked up at her father, her eyes were somber. "I think I'd rather marry a poor boy from Hebron. I could help him watch the sheep in the fields."

Eliab shook his head. "I've spoiled you badly," he murmured. "I never should have let you come out here with Benjamin and me. It isn't fitting for a girl. If I had four or five sons, I would have probably treated you as a daughter should be treated."

"I like it better this way." Abigail's voice was stubborn. "I hate weaving and spinning and grinding grain."

Eliab tried to speak firmly. "You mustn't be stubborn about doing what you're supposed to do. Come on now. It's time for you to go back home. Your mother will be frantic trying to do all the work to prepare for the feast without you there to help. You don't want to upset her, do you?"

"I'm sorry, Father," Abigail said, her words catching with a tremor. "I don't mean to be stubborn. It's just —"

Eliab nodded gently. "I know, child. You're not used to the idea of leaving home to be married. Don't think about it now. Think only about the fact that Samuel is coming. Think of it — the high priest of all Israel. Your duties to your mother should be sweetened by the thought that you're preparing food for Samuel."

He was right, of course, Abigail thought. To prepare food for Samuel was an honor, and she knew it. The high priest had never come to Hebron before. From his home in Ramah, he made an annual circuit to Mizpah, Gilgal, and Bethel. But this year, the word had come that he was traveling south

to Bethlehem and would circle down through Hebron before he headed north again; so the whole village was busy
preparing for the arrival of the high priest and his band of
nabis. Even a new altar had been hastily built on the loftiest
point in town.

"If I were a man," Abigail said, "I think I'd want to be a
nabi — a priest who served Samuel and danced and sang
before the Lord."

"Not a shepherd?" Benjamin asked with exaggerated
surprise.

Abigail only grinned at him. "Either one," she said. "A
nabi if I lived in the north — a shepherd if I lived in the
south."

"Well, you live in Hebron," her father said, "and you're
not a man but a woman with duties to perform. Get on
home then. Benjamin, see that she gets safely on her way."

"If she'll move, I will." Benjamin gave his sister a playful
shove.

Abigail swung away with a show of mock anger, but in
only a minute she was walking with reluctance toward the
village, with Benjamin at her side.

"It isn't fair," she said suddenly into the silence that had
fallen between them.

"What? That you're a woman?"

"No, not that. I don't really mind being a girl. But I do
mind that I have to marry Nabal. Mother was allowed to
marry a boy from her own village — a boy she had known all
her life. Why do I have to marry a stranger? A stranger who's
an old man?"

Benjamin didn't answer for a minute. "He's not really so
old," he began.

"You yourself said he was old," Abigail cried.

"Yes, well, old compared to you or me. But he's not forty
yet, and no doubt he'll be able to give you sons."

"But will I love him?" Abigail dared to say. "The way
Mother loves Father? You know how they look at each
other."

"As though no one else were in the room," Benjamin

agreed. "Yes, I know how it is with them. But few marriages are like that. Surely you're old enough to understand that. Think of the way old Jacob knocks his wife around. And no one seems to think there's anything wrong with that."

"I'd like mine to be just like Mother's," Abigail mourned.

"And perhaps it will." Benjamin made his voice cheerful. "You will just have to make up your mind to love him. It's as simple as that."

"You really think so?" She could not keep the skepticism out of her voice.

Benjamin hesitated. "Well, not simple perhaps. But you can make yourself do almost anything you want to do."

"I've never had to before."

"We've all spoiled you," Benjamin admitted. "Father was right about that. I'm as guilty as he is. I don't think we've made you very strong."

"I'm strong," Abigail said harshly. "You'd be surprised how strong I am." -

As they reached the edge of the village, they paused for a moment. Abigail turned her back to the square mud-brick houses to look out over the plain that stretched away from the village. She always thought of it as "the wilderness," but it wasn't a true wilderness — not the way it was in the south, where the Negeb stretched in wild, arid desolation from horizon to horizon. But it was wilderness enough for Abigail. No houses, no people, no chattering and shouting. Only the stillness of the distant sky and the changing pastel tints of the stony land — tawny gold where the rocks thrust through, lavender and blue where the shadows fell, faintly green where the pasturing places drew moisture from hidden springs.

She drew a long, shaky breath and then spoke with an odd formality. "Thank you for coming with me."

He made a farewell motion with his hand as he started to leave her. He had gone only a few steps when he turned toward Abigail again. "When I see them coming — Samuel and the nabis — when I know for sure it's them, I'll come to get you. You'll want to watch them coming across the plain."

Giving him a look of gratitude, she turned to race down the narrow street, her thin, brown legs flashing under the hem of her dark red robe. She saw women look up from their tasks in their yards, saw the look of disapproval on their faces. She knew what they were saying, that she was too old to race along the streets like this. She could almost hear the sound of their voices, like the busy clucking of the scrawny fowl that scratched in the dirt.

It's none of their business, the girl thought with defiance, but her cheeks were hot, and she felt a touch of the old perplexity that had puzzled her for so long. Why wasn't she like other girls? Why did she seem to be driven toward some unseen destiny? Would she ever be contented and serene, the way her mother was? She was aware of relief when she turned into her own house, away from the neighbors' stares.

"Where have you been?" Her mother spoke with a mixture of irritation and worry. "I've been calling and calling." There were beads of sweat along her upper lip, and her plump face was flushed with anxiety.

"A lamb got caught in a crevice too narrow for Benjamin to get into," Abigail explained. "He came to get me to fish it out."

"There are a dozen little boys in the village who could have squeezed in," Zopporah muttered.

"And not one of them intelligent enough to know how to get the lamb out without hurting it," Abigail said. "There's more to watching sheep than — than just being the right size."

Zopporah rubbed the back of her hand across her forehead with a weary gesture. "When Yahweh made women, He didn't intend them to run around and do man's work. He intended them to do what women are supposed to do."

To disagree with her, Abigail thought, would only upset her. It was better to pretend agreement. "Yes, Mother," she said meekly. "I'm sorry. But I'm here now. What do you want me to do?"

"Rub some of the dried mint in your hands, and scatter it very lightly on the clean rushes on the floor. It will make the room fragrant. And then see to it that the corn is finely ground. The slaves never make it fine enough."

Without waiting for an answer, Zopporah rushed away, moving, in spite of her bulk, like a young woman.

The next few hours passed swiftly. As Abigail worked, she filled her mind with thoughts of Samuel — memories of the stories that had been told to her ever since she had been tiny. There was no one in Israel who did not know of the virtuous woman, Hannah, who had prayed for a son and had promised to give the child to the Lord if only her desire were granted. Fathers and mothers all over the land told their children of the child, Samuel, and how he had served the old priest, Eli, with so much obedience and devotion that finally Yahweh, Himself, had called the boy by name and had revealed the future to him.

And now Samuel was coming here — the high priest whose life had been filled with mystery and honor. Abigail kept circling back to this one stupendous thought.

"Come, oh priest of Israel, come," Abigail sang softly to herself, shaping a tune in the center of her mind. No, that wasn't what she wanted to say. She needed something stronger than just the coming of Samuel, even though his presence would be a miracle.

On her knees, rubbing the grinding stone back and forth over the grain, she felt words coming in the same rhythm as her motions.

"Lead us, priest of Israel, lead." Yes, that was better. The new words would fit more closely to the tune that was already humming in her head.

There was a sudden flurry at the door, and Benjamin burst into the room. "They're coming," he panted. "I saw them coming along the ridge from the north. Come on, Abigail. Mother, may she come? I told her she could watch them coming across the plain."

Zopporah looked at her children and sighed. "Does your father permit it?"

"He told me to get her," Benjamin declared.

Zopporah looked at the eager girl. Abigail's parted lips and shining eyes held an appeal that could not be resisted.

"Then, go," Zopporah said at last. "But when they arrive, when your father goes to meet the high priest, stay well back, Abigail. Don't push to the front."

"I won't," Abigail promised. Grabbing Benjamin's hand, she tugged him toward the door. "Come on," she begged. "Oh, hurry. I can't wait!"

As she ran along beside her brother, a sudden thought came to Abigail. This was the way she ought to feel about her coming marriage. She ought to be hurrying toward the event with eager excitement. Well, she wouldn't even think about that now. Her wedding was not for three months yet. Now, she had only Samuel to think about — Samuel who would speak and dispense the blessing of Yahweh.

2

THE SHARP, PUNGENT ODOR of roasting meat drifted from the new altar and moved through the air, reaching even the women and girls who stood farthest away from the burning sacrifice. Smoke lifted in a straight, gray column and then thinned to a haze of white against the late afternoon sky. The soft chanting of the priests held a distillation of all the emotions of this gathering. Pride, praise, and petition mingled in the psalms that were chanted to Yahweh.

Abigail, who could not see Samuel from where she was, moved past the other girls and women who stood just beyond the circle of kneeling men, until the high priest was clearly in her sight. He was really here — the holy man of Israel — standing by the altar, his gray hair and beard stained crimson by the light of the fire. He looked tired, she thought, but resolute, as a man should look who had the power to anoint a king and then had revealed God's will to that king for nearly twenty years.

The chanting of the nabis rose in volume, and they moved with vigor as they stirred the fire so that the sacrifice would be more rapidly consumed. Day's end was not far away, and it was necessary that the last bone be reduced to ashes before the setting of the sun.

Abigail listened to the chanting critically. *My songs would please Yahweh better than those*, she thought. She looked around with a sudden feeling of guilt. The priests were holy men and the songs they sang would be holy songs. What right did she have to compare her own little verses with psalms which were chanted in the temple in Ramah?

And yet — in a way, it was true. Some of her songs *were* better. The one she had started while she helped her mother had burst into completion as she had stood with Benjamin, watching Samuel's arrival.

"Lead us, priest of Israel, lead.
Go before us through the night.
Give us truth, Oh blessed Samuel,
Tell us Yahweh's will for us.
We are faint and frightened — stumbling,
Groping for a hand to lead us."

She wasn't completely satisfied with it even yet. There should be more strength in the middle part. Well, she'd work on it tomorrow. Her mother complained when she slipped off to play and sing, but her father encouraged her. He liked to listen to music, he said, and since Benjamin showed no aptitude for song making, the lyre that had belonged to Eliab's father had been given to Abigail.

The fire was turning to coals, and the dusky rose of the sky was nearly the same color.

"Hear, oh children of Israel," Samuel cried out, and the nabis were silent. "Hear, oh Israel, the Lord thy God is one and Yahweh is His name."

The pronouncement was the signal for the ending of the ritualistic worship service, and the people began to gather around the high priest and his band of followers. Arrangements had been made for the nabis to be taken to the finest homes in the village, and Samuel was to be invited to the home of Eliab.

Abigail caught a compelling glance from Zopporah and, reluctantly, followed her home for the last minute preparations. The house was clean and neat, the air fragrant with the smell of new bread, roasting meat, and the herbs that had been scattered among the rushes.

"Will it be all right?" Zopporah asked anxiously.

Abigail glanced around the room, hardly seeing the plain wooden table and benches, the unadorned walls. Her mind was still on Samuel's face — fire-stained and exultant — as he had chanted the benediction. No wonder her song had seemed wrong, she reflected. She hadn't known what the man was really like. The legends hadn't prepared her for the fervor and fierceness of the old man's eyes. Nothing had prepared her for the blazing vitality of the priest's presence.

I'll need stronger words, she thought. *I'll need a tune that rings instead of sings.*

"Will it?" Zopporah asked again. "Will it be all right?"

Abigail nodded. "It'll be fine. I doubt that Samuel will even notice what he puts in his mouth."

Zopporah looked so disappointed that Abigail felt a pang of pity. "Don't worry, Mother. Father and Benjamin and the other guests will be hungry enough to make up for a whole tribe of priests."

Zopporah smiled. "I made the lentils just the way your father likes them," she confided. "With oil and leeks."

"Well, then, what else is there to worry about?" Abigail asked, unable to keep the amusement out of her voice. It really made no difference to her mother, Abigail thought, what Samuel enjoyed or didn't enjoy. If Eliab were satisfied, Zopporah would be content.

"I wouldn't want your father to be ashamed of his hospitality," Zopporah murmured.

"Father would never be ashamed of anything *you* did," Abigail assured her, finding her mother's look of gratification oddly moving.

The meal was leisurely, and the men ate with enjoyment. Perhaps Samuel was not overly concerned with what he put in his mouth, but he was obviously comfortable with these men from the tribe of Caleb. Abigail, helping her mother set steaming dishes on the table, listened avidly to everything that was being said.

"Are the king's troops still harassing the Philistines?"
Eliab asked almost casually. It was common knowledge that
Saul's men and the Philistines waged a seemingly endless
war that pushed back and forth across the long border that
separated the two nations.

Samuel's expression was sour. "It might be better to say
that the Philistines harass him. I've seen no signs of an
Israelite victory."

Eliab stopped chewing and stared at his guest. "You
mean, my lord, that the Israelite forces are truly in danger? I
hadn't heard as much."

Samuel tore at a bit of bread with his yellow teeth. "Saul is
a stubborn, bullheaded fool at times."

Benjamin looked up in amazement. "Strong words, my
lord, for the king of Israel."

Samuel stared disdainfully at the young man. "I made
him king. I can make another man king if I choose."

"But, my lord, I thought Yahweh had *told* you to anoint
him."

Samuel jerked his head around and stared in angry
astonishment at the girl who had spoken. "Who are you?"
he demanded, his voice shaking with anger.

Abigail flashed one supplicating glance at her father and
then met the priest's eyes bravely, although her knees were
shaking.

"I'm sorry, my lord. I spoke out of turn. Forgive me."

His question was repeated with asperity. "Who are you?"

"Abigail, my lord. Daughter of Eliab, sister of Benjamin.
My speech was improper."

"It was indeed." Samuel's face was grim. "Do you allow
your daughters such freedom of speech?" he shot out at
Eliab.

Eliab flushed, but his eyes gazed steadily at the high
priest. "Only one daughter, my lord. I have allowed her too
much freedom, perhaps, but she is intelligent and reverent."

Samuel turned from Eliab and stared up at the girl. "I

don't think intelligence or reverence has anything to do
with it. She is impertinent and out of place."

Abigail felt the quick, frightened pounding of her heart,
but she was able to keep her head high. As a result, she saw
what no one else saw — a flash of amusement, or was it
affection — in the old man's eyes.

"Forgive me, my lord," she said humbly and bowed her
head, but not before a quick answering smile had touched
her lips.

"Impertinent," Samuel muttered again and turned toward
Eliab. "Your daughter needs to learn her manners, my son."

Eliab spoke with an attempt at sternness. "I'll see that
she's punished, my lord."

Samuel only snorted and then turned again and glared at
Abigail. "Did I say that Yahweh did *not* speak to me about
the king? If any word is said against Saul, you may be sure it
is not *my* word."

"What has Saul done?" This time the words came from
Benjamin. "Didn't he defeat the forces of Agag? Hasn't he
served Israel well? Or has something occurred that we have
not heard about here in Hebron?"

"You are an admirer of Saul?" Samuel said.

"I am *your* admirer, my lord," Benjamin said with such
earnestness that Samuel's face softened. "Since *you* had
anointed Saul, I thought he was to be followed. I am confused, my lord."

Eliab spoke smoothly. "I and my children believe that
Yahweh speaks through His servant, Samuel. If Saul has
lost favor with our God, we want to know it."

Samuel's hard eyes seemed to strip off Eliab's and
Benjamin's flesh and lay bare their innermost being. *No one
could deceive this man; no one could disobey him and go unpunished*,
Abigail thought.

Apparently satisfied that the questions were sincere,
Samuel spoke in a confiding tone. "Indeed Saul defeated
the forces of Agag. And up to a point he obeyed my instructions. It had been a holy war, and I told him that Yahweh

demanded that all — all — of Agag's people be killed — women, children, cattle, *all.*"

Abigail felt a faint chill creep along her skin, and yet she knew that was the law. A holy war could be won only if the enemy were obliterated, not merely defeated.

"And he did not kill them?" Eliab leaned across the table, intent on Samuel's answer.

The priest's voice was spiteful. "He spared the life of Agag. For what foolish notion, I don't know. He gave me some half-hearted excuse that the king might have value to us as a hostage. And he brought the flocks home alive and healthy. To sacrifice to Yahweh, he tried to tell me. But the fact is that he disobeyed the word of his God. I *told* him what Yahweh said, and he disobeyed. I was forced to kill Agag myself."

"You, my lord?" Benjamin asked, his voice shaking.

Samuel shot a quick look at the boy. "You think I couldn't? You think Yahweh's priest can't use a sword as well as any man?"

But Benjamin's question had not come from doubt; rather, from a dawning admiration. Reverence and awe shone in his dark eyes.

"*Better* than any other man, my lord," Benjamin cried. "Yahweh would pour His strength on you and make you as strong as any youthful soldier."

Samuel relaxed and reached for another piece of bread. "Not everyone recognizes that," he muttered.

Eliab looked proudly at his son and then leaned again toward the priest. "Had he offended our God in other ways — this king of ours? Has he been other than you have told him to be?"

Samuel chewed for a minute before he spoke. "He took over the holy duties of a priest," he admitted at last. "Before I could reach his troops, he offered a sacrifice unto the Lord."

"Saul?" Eliab's voice was astonished. Who but the sons of Levi dared burn the flesh that sent up its sacred aroma to the nostrils of the Lord?

"Saul," Samuel confirmed grimly. "He has angered Yahweh so greatly that a sickness has fallen upon him."

"You mean he may die?" Benjamin gasped. "Who then would be king?"

A secretive look fled across Samuel's face, but his answer was bland. "No, there's no danger of his dying. It's not that kind of illness. His body is not sick, but he no longer carries the Spirit of Yahweh within him."

"He's mad?" Eliab breathed.

"Not quite as bad as that," Samuel said. "But when the darkness sits upon him, his household and his nation suffer."

"Is there no help for him, my lord?" Benjamin asked. "Or is it the will of Yahweh that Saul should suffer until he's no longer fit to be king?" He paused and then blurted out, "Then who would lead us?"

Samuel glanced around the table. "Later," he said wearily. "We'll discuss this later."

"You're tired from traveling, my lord," Eliab said, "and we weary you further with much talking. Come, let me lead you to our roof where a breeze blows, where you may be alone. My son and our friends will bid you farewell for now, so you can rest."

Samuel got slowly to his feet, leaning heavily on Eliab's arm. "Yes," he murmured, "I would rest for now."

Abigail watched them leave the room and head for the shallow steps that led to the open roof. *He's really old*, she thought with a sinking feeling. *I had no idea he'd be so old. I had thought he would have many, many years to lead us. But he's old.*

"Come," Zopporah said. "Carry the dishes out so the slaves can wash them. Everything went well, didn't you think so? He ate mostly bread, it's true, but your father and the other men seemed to enjoy all we had cooked. Didn't you think it went well?"

"What they *said* was more important than what they ate," Abigail said.

Zopporah looked at her daughter. "Someday, your tongue will get you in trouble," she said slowly. "You were lucky tonight that Samuel didn't demand an instant whipping for you. You've been sadly spoiled, and I suppose I'm almost as much to blame as your father."

"I didn't mean to be insolent," Abigail began, but her mother cut her off.

"You did. You think I'm a foolish old woman who cares about nothing but food and spinning. Well, let me tell you something. It's a necessary part of life that men be clothed and their bellies filled. If men are cold or hungry, they can't fight a war or compose a song or beget a child with joy. Remember that!"

Abigail stared at her mother in astonishment. "Mother, I — I'm truly sorry."

Zopporah bent her head in a gesture of reconciliation, but Abigail saw that her shoulders were stiff and unrelenting as she turned to take the dishes from the table.

"Allow me, Mother," Abigail cried and ran to take the heavier bowls from her mother's hands. "Here. You're weary. Sit down and let me carry the dishes. Don't you want to eat something first?"

Zopporah shook her head before she sat on one of the benches along the wall. "I'm too hot to eat. I'll get something later." She glanced up at her daugher. "Don't look to me for help if Samuel remembers your insolence. I tremble for you if you don't learn your place before your marriage. Perhaps a good beating *is* what you need."

Abigail pretended not to hear. She looked away from her mother's stern face and ran quickly back and forth from the dining area on the second floor to the kitchen on the ground level, snatching quick bites of food from the bowls as she ran. If she were quick and obedient and competent, Zopporah would forget her anger. This was not the right time to incur her mother's wrath. She had already called enough unfavorable attention to herself for one night. Even Benjamin had looked shocked and disapproving when she had spoken up to Samuel.

Nothing ever goes right for me, Abigail reflected, and wanted to weep with self-pity but knew she did not dare.

When the table was cleared, Abigail presented herself to her mother.

"Is there anything more you want, Mother?" she asked.

Zopporah looked up. In the dim light of the lamps, her large dark eyes were shadowed and serene. *She was never one to nurse her anger and give it permanent lodging in her heart,* Abigail thought gratefully.

"No, my child, that's all. Are you going to bed?"

"I may sit outside on the balcony for a while. It's too hot to sleep."

"Be quiet then and don't bother the men on the roof."

Abigail nodded, but after she was seated on the small balcony outside the sleeping rooms, she saw that her lyre was there, leaning against the wall.

I'll play it very, very softly, she promised herself, and took it into her arms. *No one will hear me, and maybe I'll feel better.*

Her fingers barely touched the strings, so lightly did she strum. But the chords of the song about Samuel began to shape themselves under her hands. Her voice, not much louder than a cricket's, began to sing the words.

"Lead us, priest of Israel, lead.

Go before us through the night."

The chords shifted a little, became almost militant.

"Give us truth, oh blessed Samuel,

Yahweh's truth to strengthen us."

That's better, she thought. A sudden sound above her made her look up. Samuel was leaning over the parapet of the roof, his eyes glittering in the starlight.

"You," he said. "You who are singing. Come up here. At once."

The harsh old voice held no hint of the glint of affection or amusement she thought she had detected earlier. With a sinking heart, she held her lyre against her breast and started to climb the steps that led to the roof.

3

THE ROOF OF ELIAB'S HOUSE lay in deep shadow, with small touches of light where the starlight shone on walls that would be white by day. In the corner where Eliab and Samuel sat, a small lamp burned fitfully, its flame caught and blown by the night breeze. The flickering flame threw small splashes of faint color on the faces of the two men, and it seemed to Abigail that Samuel's face was stern and unyielding. She stood well back, holding the small lyre against her body, and when she spoke her voice trembled.

"You called me, my lord?"

"I wanted to hear the song you were singing." Samuel's voice was surprisingly mild. Anticipating reprimand, she was not prepared for kindness.

"*My* song, my lord?" she asked foolishly.

"Is it *her* song?" Samuel turned to Eliab in surprise. "*She* made the song? Words and tune both?"

Although he spoke with modest words, Eliab's voice betrayed his pride. "She's only a girl, my lord. But she has been making and singing songs for most of her life."

Samuel's voice was speculative. "Odd — or perhaps more than odd — that I have found *two* young singers on this trip to the south."

"Two singers, my lord?"

But Samuel ignored Eliab's question. He turned to the girl

and spoke abruptly. "I heard my name in the song. Why did you sing about me?"

Abigail forgot her fear. "Because I've heard so much about the high priest, Samuel, the man of God. I've heard how the Lord speaks to him — and how he made a king for Israel. It seemed to me that we need men like that, my lord, so I made a song."

The light was too uncertain for her to be sure whether or not Samuel looked pleased. But his voice was kind when he said, "Let me hear it."

At first her fingers fumbled a little on the strings, and then the tune caught and steadied her. She began to sing softly and pleadingly, her voice rising in the middle of the song to intensity and then falling back again to tenderness as she sang the final words.

When she was finished, Samuel sat silently. Finally, he turned to Eliab. "You've taught her that Yahweh speaks through me?"

Eliab nodded. "Of course, my lord," he said. "I believe that Yahweh speaks to you, and you in turn speak to us. My children would absorb my convictions."

"Even a daughter?"

Was there a thread of amusement in the old man's voice? Abigail wondered. Perhaps she hadn't been mistaken about that flash of affection she thought she had seen in his eyes, after all.

"My daughter is as privy to my thoughts as my son, my lord," Eliab confessed.

Samuel didn't answer for a minute, but finally he spoke. "I mentioned the fact that I had met with two singers during this journey."

"Who was the other, my lord?" Abigail asked.

Samuel stared at her in the faint light. "David, the son of Jesse," he said. "A lad in Bethlehem."

The words were plain, but a thread of excitement colored Samuel's voice so that his listeners were sharply aware that this was not just a casual announcement.

"Should I know something about him, my lord?" Eliab's voice was carefully careless.

But Samuel seemed to welcome the question. It was obvious, even to Abigail, that he wanted to talk about the other singer from Bethlehem.

"Perhaps not. Not yet. Jesse is a man of some property and standing in Bethlehem. He has eight sons — oddly enough, one of them bears your name, Eliab. Several of the sons are soldiers in Saul's army. David is the youngest."

"He serves in the army, my lord?"

Samuel's voice was almost amused. "Not yet. He's just a boy — not much older than your daughter here. My feeling is that one day he *will* serve Saul — and be mistreated for his pains."

Neither Eliab nor Abigail spoke, but they leaned toward the old priest, intent on his words.

When Samuel continued, his voice was very calm and confident. "David will be the next king of Israel. I have already anointed him."

"The king of Israel?"

"But what of Jonathan, Saul's son?"

Eliab and Abigail spoke simultaneously, and Samuel eyed them sternly. "Jonathan may be Saul's choice. David is Yahweh's choice."

Abigail felt a curious tightening in her throat, as though she were on the verge of tears. It was a foolish reaction; she had never felt less like crying.

"But when will this take place? Does Saul know? Have you proclaimed this to the people?" The questions tumbled out of Eliab in a high, breathless sound of amazement.

Samuel actually chuckled with a sort of self-satisfaction. "I haven't told it yet — at least not to many. To a few — men who can be trusted. I'm not at all sure that even David understands."

"And he sings, you say, my lord?" Abigail's question was forced over the constriction in her throat.

Samuel stared at her, straining to see in the feeble light.

"He sings," he said. "There is no sweeter singer in the land. Not even you, my lass. But go now to your bed where you belong. Your father and I have things to discuss that are not for you to hear."

Abigail started obediently toward the steps.

"Mind," Samuel barked suddenly, "this is not for light gossip — these words you've heard tonight. If you're capable of keeping them to yourself, do so."

"I'm capable. My father will tell you that I can be trusted."

"A worthy trait," Samuel said. Again there was a faint change in his voice, as though he wanted to indulge in laughter. "A singer, a confidante, a girl who is not afraid. You have much to commend you."

"You mock me, my lord," she muttered.

"Abigail." Her father's voice was stern. "Go as you were bidden. Put up the lyre and go to bed."

"Yes, Father." With a quick nod of her head to indicate courtesy to both of the men, she backed away from them and then turned to hurry down the steps.

She lay for a long time on her mat and thought of what had been said on the rooftop. Surely, there was nothing important enough to make her heart pound. And yet, until she slept, her heart beat in sharp, quick lunges as though she were excited — or afraid.

On the rooftop, Eliab and Samuel sat in silence for a few minutes after Abigail had left, but finally Samuel spoke.

"She's an unusual girl, that daughter of yours. Beautiful to look at — evidently intelligent and even gifted. I believe I was led to your house, although I was not aware of it when I came."

Eliab felt a dryness in his throat. "What do you mean, my lord?"

"She would be a perfect wife for David when he's ready for marriage. She would bring the loyalty of your tribe — an essential thing for a young man who will be making a nation out of scattered, uncooperative tribes. She can join

him in his singing — and listen to the problems he'll have
with the people. I would think in three or four years —
perhaps sooner —"

Eliab tried desperately to interrrupt. "But, my lord —"

At first Samuel ignored him and swept on with his plans,
his conviction that he had found a wife for the young man
who would be king.

Eliab made his voice louder. "My lord, you *must* listen to
me. Please, you must listen."

Samuel stopped in amazement. "What's wrong? Haven't I
told you he will be king? Have you any idea what honor I'm
offering this daughter of yours? Why do you interrupt me?"

"Because, my lord, Abigail is already betrothed. She has
been promised to someone else. You know how binding
such promises are."

Samuel sat in a sort of stunned bewilderment. "I was so
sure," he muttered. "I felt so right about it when she came
up to the roof. Perhaps I didn't actually *hear* the voice of
Yahweh, but I felt the rightness of it all."

Eliab hesitated and then spoke humbly. "I'm more
honored than I can say, my lord. It is no small thing to have
the man of God look with favor on my daughter. A beloved
daughter, my lord. Forgive me for showing my fondness,
but I'm sure you know already how I feel about her. I would
give her to you for David, if I could. If there were any
possible way, my lord —" His voice trailed off.

"But there is no way." Samuel's words were heavy. "If
she's already betrothed, then she belongs to her husband.
David must not besmirch himself by taking what is another
man's. Well, then — I was wrong. I am very seldom wrong,
my friend," he confided suddenly. "It is not easy for me to
admit that I could be mistaken."

"Not mistaken, my lord," Eliab protested. "The idea —
the plan — was excellent. The fault lies with me — that I was
in a hurry to have her married. When a rich man came,
offering a great house and servants and many possessions,
I — I thought I should accept."

"A natural reaction, my son."

"Oh, no, my lord. Abigail, herself, was reluctant about
the marriage. I should have listened to her."

"What nonsense! One doesn't listen to a child, especially
a daughter. You did what any father would have done. If
Yahweh had really meant for David to marry Abigail, He
would have opened up the way. There will, I trust, be other
girls for him."

"Yahweh hasn't told you who, my lord?"

Samuel shook his head fretfully. "If David should go to
Saul — as I think he will — he will be exposed to Michal,
Saul's younger daughter. He'll probably think it expedient
to marry into the king's family. And Michal is a headstrong,
arrogant girl — as beautiful as she is stubborn. If she makes
up her mind to have David, he will never listen to any advice
from me."

"But surely he knows Yahweh speaks through you, my
lord?"

"Oh, yes, his head knows it. But he's a passionate young
man — handsome — eager for life. I would think that
Michal could charm him with little effort. I won't live forever, you know. Somehow, I must know that he is really firm
in his convictions before I die. That's why I had thought
that Abigail would be so perfect. Michal, you see, is not —
spiritual."

"I'm sorry, my lord."

"I, too. Well, the time is not yet anyhow. Saul is still king
and will be king until Yahweh sees fit to remove him. I
mustn't get impatient. I must trust my God and have faith."

Eliab stood and bent his head. "Will you bless me, my
lord?" he asked. "I, too, have need of faith and trust."

Samuel took Eliab's hand and pulled himself to his feet.
Putting his hand on Eliab's head, he said, "The Lord bless
you and keep you. The Lord bless this house — this tribe —
this nation of Israel."

"Will you sleep now, my lord?" Eliab suggested and led

the frail old man down the shallow, wide steps in the star-light.

Abigail's sleep was troubled. She woke frequently during the night, aware of the dreams that swam in her head. In one, she was being married. Her bridegroom stood beside her, but she could not see his face. She was conscious only of his hand on her shoulder, hard, heavy, pressing down until she cried out in pain.

In another dream, she was running across the hills, searching for one of her father's sheep, only to discover that she herself was lost, lost and threatened by the coming of night. In her sleep, she called for Benjamin, begging him to help her.

A hand touched her and woke her. Benjamin, groggy with sleep, stood beside her bed. "What are you shouting about?" he demanded. "You were shouting my name. What's wrong?"

She gasped with the sheer relief of being awake and having the dream behind her. "I'm sorry," she said. "I was dreaming. I must have been yelling in my sleep."

Benjamin turned away. "Well, if you dream again, don't call for me. Call for Mother — women don't need as much sleep as men do."

His tone was half irritated, half amused, and Abigail smiled to herself in the dark. Even sleepy and irritated, Benjamin was never unkind to her.

Her mind drifted to her dream about her wedding. The feeling of her husband's hand on her shoulder was vivid in her mind, and she found, flexing her shoulder, that there was a sore place there. She touched the tender place with fearful fingers. Had the spirit of her husband-to-be visited her in the night and dug relentless fingers into her flesh? She sat up in bed and wrapped her arms around her knees. Her wide eyes searched the darkness, but of course there was nothing to be seen.

I won't think about the dream, she promised herself. *I'll think about Samuel and the fact that he's here in this house — that he listened kindly to my song. I'll think about that and nothing else.*

But the thought of Samuel brought more than the image of his face to her mind. Samuel's words came back, sharp and clear.

"David . . . son of Jesse . . . a singer of songs. . . . He will be the king of Israel. . . . I have already anointed him."

For the first time, Abigail grasped the fact that Samuel had revealed something that very few people knew about. It was almost as though Abigail, her father, and God's prophet shared a secret.

Comforted and warmed by the thought, she lay down again and closed her eyes, courting sleep. *My dreams won't be bad if I hold the thought of Samuel in my heart,* she thought.

She was never sure, afterward, whether it was a dream or a vision that came to her in the night. It seemed as though she were on the rooftop, listening to her father and the high priest talking, although she could not understand what they said. She seemed to be crouching in a cool, dark corner, and the night wind touched her skin with a sudden chill, so that she found herself shivering with the cold.

Then she heard one word and heard it clearly. "David," Samuel said, and the echo of the word ran across the roof and through the town of Hebron and off into the hills that circled the sky.

"David . . . David . . . David." It was as though the very stars were whispering the name — as though Yahweh, Himself, had joined in the soft chant.

But what has this to do with me, the dreaming Abigail thought, shivering in her corner beyond the sight of the men. *What is it to me that the heavens and the earth whisper the name of David?*

She tried to move away and could not. She seemed to be imprisoned by some force she could not see or feel. She tried calling for Benjamin, for her father, for her mother, but her call went unanswered.

Then suddenly she called on Yahweh. Never before in her carefree life had she turned to her God with so great a need. "My Lord," she cried. "My Lord, only You can help me. Only You can save me. Only You, Lord, only You."

She felt a looseness flowing into her arms and legs and knew she was free. She turned to run away, and the quick turn wrenched her from her mat. She awoke and found herself on the cold floor, her covers pulled across her face.

Frightened, she crawled back onto the mat and lay trembling. What did the dream mean? Why had the name of David been given to her like a talisman — she, who was promised to Nabal?

Because he will one day be my king, she thought. *And perhaps I may serve him. Samuel — and Yahweh — will make him king, but there is one task that only I can do.*

Contentment and sudden sleepiness flowed over her like a wave, and she sank into the warm, safe depths of a dreamless sleep that held her until daylight.

4

AT BREAKFAST the next morning, Samuel was quiet and withdrawn. He seemed to avoid looking at Abigail, but she, caught up in the memories of the dreams that had haunted her sleep, was unaware of it. It was only when she placed a bowl of fresh milk in front of the high priest that she realized he deliberately looked away from her.

Puzzled, she backed away from the table and stared at the old man. He had looked at her with kindness last night. She was sure of it. But today he was aloof and cold.

Eliab, too, was quiet, speaking to his guest only when it was necessary. Benjamin seemed willing enough to talk, but after he had been rebuffed by the older men a few times, he lapsed into silence, shaking his head with a puzzled look at Abigail.

As the men left the table, Abigail caught at Benjamin's arm and whispered, "They must have had dreams as disturbing as mine. Yet in *my* dreams, instead of being quiet, they were talking constantly."

Samuel stopped abruptly and turned to the girl. "You dreamed about your father and me? Or did you creep back up to the roof and listen to us?"

Quick indignation made it difficult for her to be civil. "You and my father had both told me to leave the roof, my lord. I'd never disobey."

"But I heard you tell your brother that you dreamed about our talking. What were we saying?"

"I don't know, my lord. It seemed I was too far away to hear what you were saying. I heard only one word."

"And that word?"

It took courage for her to continue to look into his eyes. "The name of David, my lord." She saw him shy like a nervous donkey, and dared to say the rest. "Only the *name* of David, my lord, but it seemed as if the hills and the stars — even the sky — were whispering the name. I was frightened, my lord, and called for help, but no one came."

"And?"

She frowned, forcing herself to remember the details. "I called on Yahweh," she said. "I begged Him to — to — help me," she finished lamely, unable to express the paralysis that had held her in her dream.

"And did He help you?" The words were soft but intense.

"Yes, my lord. I was able to run away. Or I thought I was. But when I turned, I — I guess I fell off my mat." In spite of herself, she felt laughter swell in her throat.

But Samuel did not smile in response. "What do you think the dream meant?"

"How would I know, my lord? I'm not a prophetess." Then she thought of the conviction she had felt in the night. "It occurred to me when I woke up, my lord — and perhaps I should not say this to you — but it occurred to me that the dream was showing that David would really be king someday, and perhaps I would serve him in some special way."

Samuel was silent for a long minute, staring fixedly at the girl. "I wasn't so wrong, then," he finally muttered to himself. "There's something — listen, girl, do you believe that Yahweh could speak to you?"

"Oh, yes, my lord."

"Even though you're only a girl — only an ordinary girl in Hebron?"

"The lady Hannah was only a woman, my lord, but Yahweh heard her plea and gave her a son."

Samuel looked pleased. "Do you believe the dream could have been given to you for a purpose?"

Abigail waited to answer until she had arranged her words as she wanted them to be. "Yes, my lord. I think the dream was more than an announcement about David. I think the dream told me that only Yahweh could help me bear my life — the things that will happen to me. Could that be true, my lord?"

"You dreamed more than you have told me, then?"

"Yes, my lord."

His eyes softened as he continued to stare at her. "You're a brave girl," he said. "Will you kneel so I may bless you?"

She knelt obediently before him and felt the frail weight of his old hands on her head. "May the Lord bless you and give you courage, wisdom, and strength. You must remember to call on Him, and Him alone, when you need help."

This is me, Abigail thought with wonder, *and I'm being blessed by the high priest of Israel. My life will be different. I know it.*

She bent suddenly and kissed the hem of his robe, then sat back on her heels and looked up at him.

"Thank you, my lord," she whispered.

Samuel looked at her, touched her forehead again, and then turned to where Eliab stood waiting in the door.

"It only makes things worse," he muttered to his host.

Eliab nodded, casting an anxious glance at Abigail where she still knelt on the floor. She smiled reassuringly at her father and lifted a reverent hand to touch the place on her head where Samuel's hand had rested.

"Come, my lord," Benjamin called from the yard. "The nabis have all gathered, ready to continue your journey."

"I'm coming," Samuel said. "The Lord's blessings be on you and your household," he added to Eliab. He looked over at Abigail. "You won't forget to call on Yahweh?"

"No, my lord," she promised. "I won't forget."

The days after Samuel's visit seemed drab and colorless to

Abigail. The excitement of the high priest's coming, the miracle of his singling her out for conversation and blessing, had been so marvelous that everything else faded and dimmed in comparison — even the coming wedding.

Zopporah took advantage of the girl's listlessness and kept her home, indoctrinating her in the duties of women.

Indifferently, Abigail followed her mother's instructions and made more progress in the arts of weaving and spinning, cooking and cleaning than she had made in all the years before.

One day she rebelled mildly. "I don't see why I have to learn to do all this. If Nabal's as rich as you and Father say, there will surely be slaves to do all the work that needs to be done. I should be able to sit in the yard all day and play my lyre."

Zopporah looked shocked. "What a way to talk! Do you think slaves will do a task properly if the woman of the house doesn't know how it should be done? Besides, your husband may not like the sound of music. He may tell you to stop making songs."

Abigail looked at her mother with consternation. "He wouldn't. I'll — I'll *make* him let me."

"There are men who can't be *made* to do anything," Zopporah said. "Just because your father and brother are good to you, you think all men will be like that. It's not necessarily that way at all."

"You know already that he won't be like Father and Benjamin, don't you?" Abigail guessed. "Father's told you something bad about Nabal, hasn't he? That's true, isn't it?"

Zopporah flushed and looked away. "Your father never told me that Nabal would be cruel."

"Then what?"

"Nothing. Look what you're doing with that thread. You're knotting it."

Abigail sat quietly for a few minutes, picking out the knot with an unnatural patience. When the thread was smooth, she spoke in an oddly intense voice. "You'd better tell me. How will I know how to act if you don't prepare me a little?

It's not fair for you to know something I don't. I'm the one who has to marry him."

"I don't think your father —" Zopporah began.

Abigail jumped up with agitation. "What is it? I'm not a child. I have a right to know."

"He drinks," Zopporah said. "He drinks too much and gets drunk."

Abigail stared at her mother. Drunkenness was unknown in her family. Oh, there were a few men in the village who drank unwisely to ease troubles, but they were rare.

"And, knowing this, my father promised me to him?"

Zopporah spoke sternly. "Shame on you for even thinking that. Your father didn't know. Not in the beginning. It wasn't until after the contract was agreed to and signed that your father discovered what the man was like. Instead of having only one small drink to celebrate the agreement, the man drank a dozen glasses of wine. Your father said — he said Nabal was very drunk."

The words poured out as though the woman had been wanting to say them, as though she felt a sense of relief in getting them said.

Abigail turned away slowly and sat again to take up the hand spindle. "And how did he act — drunk?" she asked. "Did he become abusive — or did he just fall asleep?"

"He was — only loud, your father said. He — he was perhaps a little — vulgar."

Abigail stared at her mother, feeling the hot blood stain her cheeks. "How do you mean, vulgar?"

Zopporah kept her eyes on her spinning. "He just told some coarse jokes, I believe. Naturally your father didn't tell me what had been said."

"Naturally. And it was truly too late to break the contract?"

"Yes, too late. But don't worry too much. That isn't all of the man, surely. He's rich and clever and he longs for a son. He'll be good to you, I'm sure."

"I had a dream," Abigail confessed and stopped.

"About Nabal?"

"Yes. He hurt me."

Zopporah smiled with sympathy. "All young girls are afraid of marriage. It's nothing to be afraid of, I assure you."

Abigail looked at her mother with a touch of scorn on her face. "I'm not a fool, Mother. I've been among the sheep. I know about what is expected of a wife."

Zopporah looked distressed. "That's no way to learn about marriage — among sheep. People are different."

"In what way?" Abigail asked. "Aren't men strong like the rams, and aren't women submissive like the ewes?"

"But with men and women, there is tenderness and love. There's gentleness and joy."

Abigail looked down at her spinning. "Yes, if you're married to a man like my father. But it may not be like that for me."

"Listen to me. Your father and I had no intention of making you sad. We thought only of what would be best for you."

Abigail glanced up at her mother and then down again at the thread in her hands. All girls had to marry, and she had known since childhood that a woman's joy lay in her children, in her work. Why did she suddenly want more?

Oh, no, not suddenly, she reflected, still silent. All her life she had wanted to be happy. It was why she had coaxed to go to the fields — so that she would be free in the bright air. It was why she had made her songs, creating tunes and words to meet her great need for beauty and joy.

"Truly," Zopporah insisted. "We thought only of you."

If you had thought of me, Abigail wanted to cry out, *you would have let me be a child a little longer. You would have let me run in the fields and sing my songs and stay with Benjamin and you and Father.*

A month ago she would have said it. The hot, impetuous words would have flowed out in a quick stream of pain. But she was not the same girl she had been a month ago. She had dreamed dreams sent by Yahweh; she had been blessed by Samuel.

"It's all right, Mother," she said soothingly. "Don't worry. It'll be all right."

Her mother sighed with relief. "I only want you to be happy," she said.

Abigail nodded. "I know. Honestly, Mother, I know."

But what will I do, she thought, *if he gets drunk and beats me or says vile things to me? What will I do then?*

5

A FEW WEEKS LATER, a messenger arrived from Maon with a message from Nabal.

"My master says the little house, prepared for the bride, is ready," the man announced.

Eliab nodded heavily. If Abigail's groom had been a resident of Hebron, things would have been simpler. On the day chosen for the wedding, she would have merely waited in her father's house until her groom came to take her away from her feasting, celebrating relatives.

But Nabal was not from Hebron, so in an attempt to follow tradition and yet not require too much traveling for anyone, Nabal had said he would prepare a small house midway between Hebron and Maon for the bride's family to use.

"Tell your master," Eliab boomed in an attempt to be as jovial as he should be, "that the bride and her family will leave here early tomorrow. Tell him that we'll have our marriage feast in the little house and that he may come there for his bride soon after midday of the following day."

Nabal's servant, refreshed by food and drink, nodded politely. "I will deliver the message, my lord," he said to Eliab. Just before he mounted his horse, his eyes darted across the yard to where Abigail and Zopporah stood modestly in the shade of the porch. He looked away again immediately, but not before Eliab had seen a flash of pity in the man's eyes.

It's only the pity all men feel for young girls going to older men, Eliab tried to tell himself, but his heart was heavy. *When a man has only one daughter,* he thought with grief, *when she is still a child in some ways, giving her up is hard. I can only hope that the drunkard I saw the night we signed the contract was not Nabal's true self.*

There was nothing to be done about it, of course. *Yahweh will have to protect her,* he thought, and turned his attention to the messenger, waiting on the horse.

"Tell him we'll leave here at dawn," Eliab said, and slapped the horse's flank so that it pranced sideways. Used to donkeys and their deliberate movements, Eliab was not prepared for the quick skittishness of the beast.

There will be much to get used to, Eliab reflected, and watched Nabal's servant ride away. Even when the sound of hoofs had dwindled to silence, Eliab did not turn to where his wife and daughter stood.

"I must go to the sheep," Eliab said. He walked away sullenly, engulfed in his misery.

Zopporah turned to face Abigail. "So it's tomorrow," she said. "I had hoped for another day or two. I'm not sure I can be ready."

Abigail smiled, trying to ignore the hollow feeling in her stomach. "Don't worry, Mother. You always worry and you always get everything done."

"Have you packed everything you plan to take?"

"Yes. The clothes and things are in the large basket you gave me to use. My lyre is wrapped in heavy cloth."

"You won't need weaving or baking tools," Zopporah said. "But we've discussed all this before."

"Yes." Abigail's voice was tight. "His first wife would have had everything. I understand that."

Nothing of my own, she grieved silently. *Everything already handled and used — by a stranger. It would be different if they were things my mother had used.*

"Then — then — what do you want to do now?" Zopporah seemed unable to look directly at her daughter. "I — it seems that there must be a hundred things to do — now that the day has actually come. But I don't know what to suggest."

Abigail took quick advantage of her mother's hesitation. "May I go out to the fields where Benjamin is? Just one last time? Please, Mother."

Zopporah looked anxious. "You'll get all scratched up again. I've just got your bruises and cuts all healed during the past week. I wouldn't want you to go to your husband looking like an outlaw."

Abigail forced a light laugh. "No, I won't. I promise. I'll only sit and talk — and watch the light across the valley. Even if our best ewe gets caught, I won't help. I'll only be with the sheep for one last time."

"Nabal has thousands of sheep."

"And even if he brought an injured lamb home, do you think it would be to his wife he'd bring it? In a house as rich as they say his house is?"

"I suppose not," Zopporah conceded. "But you *will* be careful?"

"I promise."

"Then go. I understand how you feel. Even just going to your father's parents' house, across the village, seemed a terrifying thing to me. I remember how I went and sat on the roof of our house, and how I kept touching it as though I'd never see it again. It's a foolish thing, but I suppose all girls are alike."

Abigail flung her arms around her mother's neck. They did not often touch, and so the movement was an unexpected one.

"Thank you," Abigail whispered. She turned away quickly and ran out of the house.

Emerging from the shelter provided by the houses of Hebron, Abigail stepped out into the unprotected open plain. For a few minutes she stood quietly, feeling the tug and pull of the wind. Her robe and head scarf whipped about her body and face, but she welcomed the wild buffeting. *This is what I love*, she thought. *This is what I wish I could always have.*

Far across the slanting land, she saw the gray specks that were her father's sheep. The small black figure under the widest tree would be Benjamin, of course. He would depend on the boys watching the sheep to call him if a problem developed. *Dear, dear Benjamin*, she thought fondly. He was really too indolent to look for problems himself.

She started running toward him, delighting in the sun on her face and the wind in her hair. Benjamin apparently had seen her coming, so he was sitting up, waiting for her. Excitement lit up his face. "How did you escape?" he asked.

"Nabal's servant came. Everything's ready and we leave tomorrow." Her voice was flat and expressionless.

"Tomorrow. I had thought maybe not until next week."

"I know." She dropped beside him on the ground. "You look as though you had just seen an angel fly by. What happened?"

Benjamin grinned. "I didn't know everything showed in my face. I just heard something exciting this morning — that's all."

"What?" Maybe he could take her mind off tomorrow.

"A wandering soldier came by," Benjamin confided. "Or at least he said he was a soldier. To tell you the truth, I think he's running away from Saul's army. I don't know. But he told me a story that's almost unbelievable."

"Maybe he's a liar," she suggested.

"Probably. But not about this. He had seen it and he was telling the truth. You can tell about things like that."

"Well, tell me," she said impatiently.

"He was with Saul's army at the valley of Elah," Benjamin recounted, his eyes shining, "and he said that the Philistines sent a huge soldier out every day to challenge them."

"How huge?" Abigail's voice was skeptical in spite of her brother's enthusiasm.

Benjamin shot her a withering glance. "He was a span taller than six cubits," he said. Seeing the disbelief in her eyes, he spoke more aggressively. "He was! They were speaking of him as a giant, and not one man in Saul's army dared to answer the challenge."

"Not even the soldier who told you the story?" Abigail asked.

"No, not even him. Doesn't that have a ring of truth to you? What man would admit his own cowardice if he planned to lie? He would have made *himself* the hero, wouldn't he?"

"You mean there's a hero?" Her voice was casual, her attention not yet wholly fastened on her brother's story.

"Yes, and you've heard about him. When Samuel was here, he told you and Father that he's already anointed him as Israel's next king. Remember? David of Bethlehem."

The name went through her with the quick, bright pain of a knife slash, but she held herself quiet. "Well, what about this hero — this David?" she said as calmly as possible. "What did he do?"

"He killed him. David killed the giant, Goliath, with a slingshot."

Abigail stared at her brother. "Just like that? With a slingshot? A giant? Oh, Benjamin!" She had hoped her voice would be filled with scorn, but there was a waver in the tone that she didn't like.

Benjamin didn't seem to notice. "Yes. Now, listen. David had come down from Bethlehem — to visit his brothers in the army — and when Goliath came out with his usual boast that no one dared to fight him, David volunteered to go out against him."

Seeing that his sister's attention was fully on him at last, Benjamin went on eagerly. "They offered him armor — weapons — everything. But he simply took his slingshot."

Unconsciously, Benjamin's hand went to the leather pouch with its long thong that was always in his belt. No shepherd would be without one, of course, and Abigail had seen too many smooth pebbles flung wickedly from the swirling slings to doubt their lethal power.

"Didn't the giant use his club or knife?" she asked.

"David never let him get that close," Benjamin said. "He stood well back — probably looking like a harmless boy to Goliath — and he fitted a pebble to the sling and shot the enemy squarely in the middle of his forehead."

"It killed him?"

"No, of course not. But it stunned him, and David ran in and used the giant's own sword and killed him and cut off his head."

There was a brief silence while the two sat looking at each other. Abigail could hear the labored sound of her breath as it sawed in and out.

When she spoke, the words were not at all what she intended to say. They came with as much surprise to her as to Benjamin. "And did he give Yahweh the glory? Did he kill Goliath with the name of the Lord on his lips?"

Benjamin stared at his sister. "Yes," he said, his words almost a whisper. "How did you know? He said the victory would be given to him that all the world would know there was a God in Israel."

"I don't know how I knew," Abigail confessed. "I just knew. And will David be with Saul's army now?"

"More than Saul's *army*. He's part of Saul's household, the man said. A close friend of Jonathan — and who knows? perhaps he'll be even a closer friend to one of Saul's daughters. There are two, I understand. Merab and Michal. Perhaps Saul will give one of them to David out of gratitude."

A peculiar wave of coldness seemed to be drowning Abigail all at once. *But what of me*, some strange, lost voice seemed to be crying. *If David loves the daughters of a king, what about me?*

"Are you all right?" Benjamin's voice seemed to be coming from far away.

She drew herself out of the dark wave. "I'm fine," she said slowly. "The running — and the heat — and knowing that tomorrow —"

Her voice trailed off and her brother leaned toward her solicitously. "Here, take a drink of water. And eat a fig or two. You know you shouldn't run in this heat."

She drank the water and ate the fig obediently. Then she drew a long, shuddering sigh. "I'll miss you, Benjamin. I'll miss you, I think, more than anyone."

"But I plan to see you often," Benjamin announced. "The journey is less than two days — and Father has promised me that I may come your way several times a year. I don't think I could stand it, not seeing you."

It was the closest he had ever come to speaking of his affection, and she stared at him with delight. "Oh, Benjamin, I can stand anything now. It was not seeing you again — you and Mother and Father — and this countryside and our house —"

Words failed her and she leaned against her brother in silent despair. He had no words to comfort her, apparently, but his hands smoothed her hair gently and finally he kissed her cheek.

"All girls act like this when they're getting married," he said as though he were an authority. "But think of all the good things your life will hold. You'll have a rich house and a husband who will love you —" Her sharp movement stopped him, but he went on doggedly. "He will, Abigail, he will. He can't help it. Even if he — even if he isn't always what you want him to be, he'll love you, I'm sure of it."

She had thought only of whether or not she would love Nabal. She hadn't really given any thought to whether or not the man would love her. She sat quietly beside her brother, thinking. Her father and her brother were gentle and kind because they loved her. Well, then, if she were very lovable, perhaps Nabal would do the same. It was a new idea and she turned it over and over in her mind, examining all sides of it.

"I didn't say anything wrong, did I," Benjamin asked anxiously.

"No, you said the very words I needed most. You're a good brother, Benjamin. You've given me something to think about — and if I can count on your coming to see me sometime, then — then I can do anything."

"Wonderful!" he applauded. "Come on, it's nearing sunset and I see the boys are rounding up the sheep for the night. Shall we race home? One last time?"

She nodded eagerly and scrambled to her feet. She listened to her brother's shouted instructions to the boys, and all the time her thoughts were racing. The time had come to stop mourning for what could not be. The time had come to step out, armed only with her small weapon of will. *If David can kill Goliath,* she thought, *then maybe I can do — whatever it is I have to do.*

"Go!" Benjamin shouted in her ear, and they began their race for home.

Not until she lay on her own sleeping mat did Abigail's thoughts go back to that minute on the hillside when Benjamin had said, "Perhaps Saul will give one of them to David out of gratitude." The dark feeling that had choked her then had been almost evil.

What did you want, some hard, honest little voice asked. *Did you want David for yourself?*

I am going to marry Nabal, Abigail thought with sturdy reality. *Tomorrow I will leave this place to become Nabal's wife.*

She was nearly asleep when a final thought came to her. *I will be so good a wife,* she thought, *that all the earth will know there is a God in Israel.* With David's words in her mind, she fell asleep.

6

IT WAS ABIGAIL herself who caught the first glimpse of Nabal and his followers coming, at a fast trot, toward the small building where the tribesmen of Eliab were making merry in celebration of the marriage of one of their daughters.

"Mother," Abigail's voice was breathless. "Look, he's coming."

Zopporah squinted in the direction that Abigail was pointing. "You can see better than I," Zopporah said. "Wait, I'll tell your father."

She hurried to where her husband sat with his brothers and cousins and whispered in his ear, and then she came back to Abigail. With unsteady hands, she placed the garland of almond blossoms, kept fresh in a basket under wet cloths, on Abigail's head. Then, gently, she pulled the thin, orange shawl that had been around the girl's shoulders up over her hair and draped it across her face.

"Sit under the little tent," she said. "It's where you're supposed to be when he comes."

Abigail, watching the cloud of riders approaching, was reminded of the day she and Benjamin had seen Samuel and the nabis coming down from the north. What was it that Samuel had said to her? That she must call on Yahweh and on Him alone when she needed help. Well, she needed help now. If she were going to be able to leave her family with a smile, Yahweh would have to show her how.

The flurry of horses' feet and the welcoming cries of the Calebite men drowned out her own thoughts. Staring silently at the floor, feeling the heat of blood in her cheeks, she sat and waited.

Greetings were exchanged and toasts were drunk by the eager, laughing men. Abigail could hear even Benjamin's and Eliab's voices crying out with the joyful acclamation of "To life!" Her mother was busy pouring wine and offering small, rich cakes. It seemed, for a moment, as though she were totally alone, sitting in the middle of the small tent, blinded by the shawl that fluttered around her face, half smothered by the over-sweet scent of the almond blossoms.

She felt a light touch on her elbow and turned, startled, to see, mistily through the veil, a dark-skinned girl crouching beside her.

"My lady," the girl said softly. "I am Rachel — brought by my lord, Nabal, to serve you."

Abigail lifted her veil momentarily and looked into the vivid face so close to her own. The girl was as small as Abigail was, darker, with hair that curled damply around her face in spite of the scarf that attempted to bind it closely to her head.

Abigail felt a curious lightening of the oppression that had held her for such a long time. Here was someone for her comfort. *One's prayers are not usually so quickly granted*, Abigail thought with a touch of her old humor.

"My husband could not have provided anything I needed or wanted more," Abigail confessed to the girl. She saw the delight that filled Rachel's dark eyes. "You won't leave me?"

"From this moment on," Rachel promised. "I'll be as near to you as I can be — doing anything you want me to do."

With a small sigh of relief, Abigail smiled at the girl and then turned to find herself face to face with the man she knew must be Nabal.

She felt her heart quicken, but not with the feeling of fear she had anticipated. The moment itself was not so dreadful as she had thought it would be.

"My lord," she said quietly.

"Will you come?" he said.

She tried to see him through the filmy folds of the scarf, but dared not lift it for even one clear peek. Through the orange haze of her veil, she saw only that he was shorter than her brother or father, that his face was round and soft.

"Yes, my lord. I will come."

It was the prescribed answer to a question that had been asked out of formality. She had no choice, and both of them knew it.

There was quick laughter and calls of congratulations as Nabal took Abigail's hand and pulled her to her feet. Small glasses of wine were thrust into their hands and a sudden hush fell.

"To life, then," Eliab said loudly, "a life of blessing and honor."

"To life," Nabal responded, and drank.

Abigail pulled the veil away from her mouth, lifted her glass, and drank briefly. She felt the glass taken from her fingers and realized it was her mother beside her.

"May the Lord bless you," Zopporah said. "Go with our blessing and our love."

Eliab came up next, his hands trembling a little as he took Abigail's fingers in his. "Be obedient to your husband," he said. "Be fruitful and multiply and bring honor to your father's house."

She blinked quickly so the sudden tears would not fall. "I'll be everything you taught me to be, Father."

All the family began to crowd around them, and for a little while Nabal stood patiently, letting Abigail's relatives wish them well. But long before they had all spoken their words of blessing and congratulations, he had become impatient.

"Enough," he cried. "We have a long way to travel. Would you have me keep my bride out after darkness has fallen, so that we would be in danger of bandits?"

Confused and apologetic, they began to move away, but Benjamin persisted in pushing to the front.

"But she is my sister, sir," he protested, laughing good-naturedly. "You won't deny me the right to bid her farewell?"

Nabal did not laugh. Instead, his voice was hard. "Hurry, then. We haven't time to waste on foolishness."

A sudden anger touched Abigail, but before she could say or do anything to reveal her feelings, Benjamin was close to her, gripping her hands in both of his.

Although his voice was light and almost merry, Abigail could feel the rigidity of his fingers. "No, then, he's right, my sister. Long farewells are foolish. Here, take my kiss and go with your husband."

He bent to her cheek but his voice breathed in her ear. "Be brave, little one. I'll come soon."

"Good-bye, Benjamin," she said steadily and clearly. "We'll look for your visit some day in the future."

"You plan to come our way?" Nabal's voice was cold.

"Whenever Yahweh leads me in the direction of Maon," Benjamin replied, his voice still cheerful.

Nabal did not answer. He made a sweeping gesture that seemed to push Eliab's family away. "We go, then," he announced. "You will ride behind me," he said to Abigail. "Have you ever ridden on a horse?"

"No, my lord."

"Are you afraid?"

Her voice was scornful. "No, my lord."

Deftly, Rachel pulled Abigail's robe between her legs, tucking the hem snugly into the girdle that hugged her waist.

When Nabal was on his horse, one of his servants, a tall, burly fellow, lifted Abigail as though she were a child and placed her behind her new husband.

Before the others could mount, before further good-byes could be said, Nabal had kicked his heels into the horse's sides, and they were pounding away from the small house that sheltered the family of the bride.

She had never in her life traveled this fast before. The servant had wrapped her arms securely about Nabal's waist, so she felt absolutely no fear at all. The air whipped against her face, blowing the concealing scarf away and pulling it against her throat so that its ends flew out behind her.

In spite of her grief at leaving her parents and Benjamin, she could not suppress the elation that filled her as the horse galloped across the sand. It had nothing at all to do with the man in front of her. It was simply the speed and the wind in her face. In spite of herself, laughter bubbled up in her throat.

Nabal turned his head to glance at her with disbelief. "Are you laughing — or crying?"

"Laughing, my lord. I've never ridden like this before. It's the excitement of going so fast."

A look of satisfaction spread across Nabal's face. "I can go faster," he said in the boasting tone of a boy.

"Truly, my lord?"

In answer, he brought the small whip he carried down across the horse's side, and the animal lengthened its stride until it seemed to Abigail she must be flying.

For a few minutes, the sensation was purely delicious, but the excitement and unaccustomed movement began to whirl in Abigail's head until she felt a strange dizziness growing in her.

"Please, my lord," she gasped, furious with herself for her weakness. "I'm getting dizzy. I'm not used to it, you know. Could you slow the horse now?"

She felt his hesitation even with his back toward her. She saw the start of another motion of his whip hand and felt the reluctance with which he stopped the arm in midair.

There was impatience in his voice when he said, "So you are like all women, after all — timid and weak."

Stung, she cried out, "I am not. It's just — this has been a difficult day — I had never ridden fast before. If you want to race the horse, go ahead."

"You forgot the 'my lord,'" he said.

"Go ahead, my lord."

He pulled on the reins until the horse had settled to a walk. His laugh was filled with self-satisfaction. "Why should I run the risk of making you angry or sick?" he said, turning his head to look at her over his shoulder. "I want a happy, healthy bride when I take you to my bed tonight."

She felt shock run through her at his frankness, but she did not lower her eyes when he glanced back at her.

"You're really quite beautiful," he said, turning again for another quick glance. He used the same tone her father used to discuss the merits of a good sheep. "I hadn't known you were quite so beautiful."

He pressed his arms down over her arms and pulled her closer to him. "Come, I'm more anxious than ever to get home. Will you fall off if I make the horse trot?"

Her pride stiffened. "Go as fast as you like, my lord. I'm quite recovered from my faintness."

But he kept the horse at a moderate speed, and before long his servants had caught up to them. The tall servant who had lifted Abigail cantered up beside them, and Abigail saw that Rachel was sitting behind him. The girls looked at each other, smiling, but exchanged no word. Except for a few words of instruction from Nabal, the rest of the ride was made in silence.

It was dusk when they rode up a small hill to where a wall ran around a large plot of ground. Behind the wall, Abigail could see the bulk of a house against the purple sky.

"Here we are," Nabal announced. "Here is my house."

The yard surrounding the house was wide, the dirt packed down firmly, with many trees growing along the wall. The house itself was at least twice as large as Eliab's house — whitewashed and solid — with the soft gold of oil lamps spilling out the open doors.

Abigail, staring, felt hard hands go around her waist and felt herself being lifted to the ground. For a few seconds, her legs were limber with weakness and the ground seemed to tilt under her feet.

Rachel was suddenly beside her. "Come, my lady," she said. "I'll show you to your room so that you can refresh yourself and get ready for the evening meal."

"There will be no festivities," Nabal announced from above her in the dusk. "You and I will merely have a small meal in your room. Rachel, see that someone serves it."

"Yes, my lord. When my lady is ready, I'll call you."

"Make it quick," Nabal said as he swung down from his horse. "I've waited long enough for this night."

There was a leer on his face as he glanced at one of his servants. Without even looking to see if the man responded to his master, Abigail followed Rachel across the yard and into one of the doorways. They crossed a large room, evidently a sitting room, furnished with chairs and divans covered with rich-looking cloth, and went up a narrow stairway to an upper hallway. The hall opened onto several rooms which must have been on the eastern side of the house, as they felt cool and breezy.

Rachel led the way to the largest room. "Here," she said. "This is where you'll sleep, my lady. There's a basin of water there beyond that screen. I'll bathe you — I'm sure you're dusty from the ride — and see, here's a robe the master has provided for you."

Abigail glanced at the robe lying on a chair. It was made of a deep blue stuff with gold threads worked into the hem and the edges of the sleeves. She had never seen anything so lovely.

"I've never been washed by anyone before," she confessed shyly, half unwilling to step out of her dusty dress.

But Rachel was very matter-of-fact. "You'll get used to it, my lady. When you have a husband as wealthy as my lord, you learn to take things like this for granted."

Rachel was skillful and discreet, and Abigail felt no embarrassment during the process of being bathed and dressed. It was only when she pulled the new robe over her head that she discovered it was much too large for her. The sleeves fell over her hands and the hem touched the floor.

"We'll put it up with a girdle," Rachel decided, looking at Abigail with her head tilted to one side. "I guess my lord had forgotten how big his first —" Her words stumbled to a stop, her cheeks red with confusion.

"This was his first wife's, then?" Abigail asked coolly.

"It came from Mesopatamia," Rachel said as though that explained everything.

"If my own clothes were unpacked, I would wear something of my own," Abigail said, "even though it only came from Hebron."

Rachel gave a quick, nervous glance over her shoulder. "No, no, my lady. It's far better to wear what he has provided. Here, I'll tie this securely around your waist — see? Then if I pull the robe up, it will clear the floor nicely. Can you manage the sleeves, do you think?"

"I could fold them up," Abigail said, "but then the gold wouldn't show. And I'm sure he wants the gold to show, doesn't he?"

"Yes, my lady," Rachel whispered, and the eyes of the two girls met with perfect understanding.

"Then I'll manage," Abigail said abruptly.

After Rachel had brushed Abigail's hair, leaving it hanging loosely over her shoulders, she started toward the door.

"I'll call him," she said. "I know he's anxious. Will you be all right, my lady?"

No, oh, no, Abigail wanted to say. *Stay with me.* But she said nothing.

Just then, two servants came in with a basket of fruit, some wine, and a flat loaf of bread. They placed the food on a small table, trying not to look at Abigail with curiosity.

"Will it be enough, my lady?" one of them asked.

"Oh, yes, plenty. I'm not really hungry."

"And a good thing," Nabal announced from the doorway.

"Who wants food on such a night? Leave us now and don't disturb us again."

Rachel and the other servants ducked their heads in mute agreement and scuttled away. Abigail, her heart pounding, watched her husband come toward her across the room.

"Do you like the robe?" he demanded.

"Yes, my lord, It's — it's lovely."

"It's too big," he discovered. "Someone will have to alter it. Oh, well, it doesn't matter. Come here."

She started obediently toward him and felt her face grow hot under the possessiveness of his eyes as they strayed from her face to her throat. She felt his arms go around her and was momentarily aware of the sourness of his breath as his lips fumbled moistly, seeking hers.

Oh, Yahweh, she prayed in silent desperation, *help me now.* The prayer was swallowed up by the realization that she was a woman who had a duty to perform. Yahweh had laid down His laws and expected her to obey.

Somehow, she kept herself erect and did not flinch away from her husband's kiss.

7

THE MORNING LIGHT slipped so gently into the room that Abigail awoke with a feeling of peace. At first, she believed she was at home, and that the sounds she heard through the window were the sounds of Hebron. Gradually, she became aware of the presence of Nabal, certain, even before she looked at him, that he was watching her.

His light brown eyes were filled with satisfaction underlaid with curiosity or speculation.

As soon as she glanced at him, he announced, "You didn't weep."

"Why should I weep?" She forced herself to say the words in a voice as expressionless as his. *If I had felt like weeping,* she thought, *I wouldn't let him know.*

"All girls weep," he said. "Or at least my first wife did."

I could flatter him, she thought coldly. *I could say he has acquired skill with the passing of the years. But it would be a lie. He knows nothing of the gentleness and joy my mother spoke of. He's a fool.*

Her scorn was like a rod of iron up her back. "I'm not the sort of girl who weeps, my lord," she said in a stiff voice. "I hope this does not displease you."

For a moment he did not answer. Then, affecting a fond smile, he said smoothly, "You are too new and too young to either please or displease me. We'll see whether or not you behave as I want you to."

"I know it's my duty to obey you, my lord. My father and my mother taught me that at least."

"Your father and your mother spoiled you," he said abruptly. He turned and got up from the mat. "I didn't take you with my eyes shut. I know you were allowed ridiculous freedom. Things will be different here. Be sure of that. I'm not as foolish as your father."

"I am new to your house, my lord," she said, holding her chin steady. "You will forgive me if I still feel loyalty to my father's house?"

He turned to look at her. "You'll get over that," he said indifferently. "When you have my child, you'll forget about Hebron." He started away and then swung back to her. "Do you plan to just lie there all day?"

For a second, she felt her blood rise in her face at the thought of getting up with a man in the room. With a deft movement, she wrapped the woven bed cover around her body and stood up.

"Your modesty becomes you, my love," Nabal said, suppressing laughter.

She lowered her lids so that her anger would not show in her eyes. "Thank you, my lord. Will Rachel come to help me dress?"

This time, Nabal laughed outright, but there was admiration in his laughter. "You learn the ways of rich men rapidly, my girl." He belted his robe tightly before he started for the door. "I'll send her up. You can spend the day getting acquainted with the house and the servants. Since this is not a first marriage, work will go on as usual. I'll be away most of the day."

She felt a quick lifting of the heart. "As you say, my lord."

"Take your time. The maids will have breakfast ready for me and my men. You can eat later with my aunt and the other women."

She watched him leave the room, then turned away. She really had not expected the feeling of aversion that churned coldly through her stomach when she thought of the night just past. She hadn't expected pleasure, but she hadn't dreamed that she would feel violated and outraged. She walked to the window, trailing the bed cover behind her. She was probably being stupid. The man was her husband, and, after all, he had not been cruel. He had simply been insensitive, casual, unaware of her as a person.

She thought of her worry over whether or not she would love her husband, and of her vow to make him love her. In the light of this morning, both thoughts seemed childish. She would learn to live without love.

A sound at the door took Abigail's attention from the window. Rachel, carrying a basin of steaming, fragrant water, a soft cloth over her arm, stood in the doorway.

"May I bathe you now, my lady?"

Abigail smiled. "Have you found my clothes from home?"

"Yes, my lady. I have them ready. Your red robe, perhaps, and the blue-striped scarf for your head?"

"Fine. And when I've eaten, you'll show me the house and the land around it?"

Rachel set down her basin. "Oh, yes, my lady." Her eyes, warm and anxious, looked directly into Abigail's. "You're all right, my lady?"

For just a second, the girl's compassion weakened Abigail's rigid control. "Of course," she responded, but her voice wobbled briefly. "You may see me weep — out of home-sickness, perhaps, or some other grief. But I don't snivel over the ordinary things in life."

Rachel smiled. "I'm not surprised, my lady. Now, come, and let me wash you. By the time we're finished, the men will be gone."

Abigail had anticipated a day that would drag, heavy with homesickness and dread of the coming night. Amazingly, this was not true at all. She found Nabal's aunt, Topeleth, to be a gentle, shy, motherly woman who seemed willing to show the girl the workings of the house and gave no indication that she was jealous of a new mistress.

"You're too young to be responsible for everything all at once," Topeleth said in a soft, comfortable voice. "Time enough when the babies come to spend all your time working. Just now, you ought to be a little bit free."

Abigail gazed at the older woman in delight. "Then you won't mind if sometimes I play my lyre and sing my songs?"

Topeleth nodded. "Why not? Just — well, it might be better to do it when our lord Nabal is not home."

"He doesn't like music," Abigail guessed.

"There are many things he doesn't like."

"Did he and his first wife — are there no children?" Abigail asked. She had asked the question of her parents, but they had been unable to answer, and she had forgotten to ask Rachel.

"There were three babies, but they sickened and died." There was honest grief in the faded, old eyes.

Abigail felt a swift pang of pity for the first wife who had wept on her wedding night and had died childless. "Well," she said, "perhaps Yahweh will give this house a son at last."

Topeleth beamed. "This house is in need of a son," she said.

Abigail dropped her eyes. "I'm the slave of Yahweh," she murmured. "May He grant me blessing."

Topeleth dabbed at her eyes, patted Abigail's arm affectionately, and hurried to the kitchen to oversee the work there. Abigail turned to the steps that led to her room.

I'll get my lyre, she decided. *I'll find a shady spot and rest my bones that ache so from that ride yesterday, and I'll comfort myself with some songs.*

Seated in the shade, she plucked the strings gently until the music caught her. She sang some of the old songs that had been part of her childhood, finding comfort in the familiar words. She was, in fact, so absorbed in her music that she was hardly aware of the passing hours.

Rachel came around the corner of the house.

"You sing beautifully, my lady," she said. "Whose songs are you singing?"

"My own," Abigail answered, not even looking up from the strings she was plucking. "Most of them, that is."

Rachel's voice was filled with wonder. "You made the songs, my lady? But you're only a girl."

"Yahweh gave me songs from my cradle. My father gave me the lyre."

Rachel squatted down beside her. "May I listen?"

"Of course. Here's a song I used to sing to quiet the sheep." She crooned a short lullaby, weaving a spell of serenity and peace.

"It's lovely," Rachel cried. "A singer of songs came through here only a few weeks ago — a boy from Gibeah, the town of King Saul. He sang a song so exciting that I learned it. Would you like to hear it, my lady?"

Abigail smiled. "Of course. Is the song about Saul?"

"In a way. It goes like this. Listen." The girl's voice was husky and not really true, but the words rang with conviction. "Saul has slain his thousands," Rachel sang, "and David has slain his tens of thousands."

Abigail felt the familiar kick in her heart. Every time she heard of this David, there was the same reaction — as though she were encountering something both precious and frightening.

She allowed none of this to show in her voice. "I'm not surprised that the singer of that song left Saul's court. Surely the king would be angered by it. It must have been sung only in secrecy — by friends of this — this David."

Rachel shook her head emphatically. "The singer said that girls were singing it in the streets — dancing, he said, in honor of Saul and David. Particularly of David."

"And David's not in danger?"

Rachel looked puzzled. "Why would he be in danger, my lady?"

Abigail had a sudden memory of the strongest rams fighting to determine who would be leader of the pack of sheep. It would be that way with men, too. Surely it would.

"Sing it again," she said to Rachel. "I want to learn it."

Obediently, Rachel began the song. After she had heard

the words a few times, Abigail began to search for the chords on her lyre. In a short time, she had mastered the melody and she began to sing it, accompanying herself with plucked chords.

"What are you singing?"

The voice was Nabal's, and Abigail nearly dropped the lyre.

"My lord," she gasped. "You're home. I didn't hear you come."

"Obviously, or you would have been waiting for me in a more appropriate place than the yard. I ask you again — what song were you singing?"

"It's a song about King Saul, my lord," she said.

"It didn't sound like that to me," Nabal shot back at her. "It sounded more like a song about that upstart, David the Bethlehemite. Sing it again."

She obeyed, singing the words clearly in spite of the fact that her heart was pounding.

"Just as I thought," Nabal barked. "It's an insult to the king. I forbid you to sing it again. Do you hear me?"

In spite of a quick flare of anger, she was able to answer with a docile voice. "Of course, my lord. If that is your wish."

Nabal narrowed his eyes in quick surprise before a look of self-satisfaction deepened into a silky smile. "I expected you to be different. Could it be that in only one night I have tamed you?"

"In one *day*, my lord," she corrected him. "I am impressed with your aunt and your house and —" she flicked a quick look at Rachel who had been cowering in fear ever since Nabal arrived "— and your servants. Why should I be unpleasant to my lord?"

"Why indeed?" Nabal said smugly. "So put away your toy and come and help my aunt prepare my dinner. It will be better if your hands have handled it."

"Certainly, my lord. If you'll excuse me long enough to run up to my room with the lyre."

"Rachel can do it," he insisted.

"It takes two, my lord, to wrap it properly." Her voice was soft but firm.

He stared at her for a few seconds before he shrugged and turned on his heel. "Suit yourself," he said. "Only don't keep me waiting."

Rachel came, as silent as a shadow, at Abigail's heels. When they had gained the privacy of Abigail's room, she whispered, "You didn't blame me, my lady. You didn't tell him I had taught you the song."

"Why should I?" Abigail asked absently, heady with her first small victory.

"Most women would have," Rachel said. "I'm grateful, my lady." Her hands were busy helping with the folds of the cloth. "You will sing the song again, won't you, my lady?" she asked suddenly, lifting her head to look at her mistress.

Abigail knew what she *ought* to say. Instead, she said flatly, "Yes, I will sing it again."

Rachel's eyes shone with adoration. "And when I can, my lady, I'll tell you about this David — about how he killed the Philistines who are the enemies of the Lord God — and how he won Michal, the king's daughter, to be his bride."

"Yes," Abigail said, turning away so that Rachel would not see her face. "Yes, when we're alone, you may tell me all you know. But for now, I must hurry to serve my husband. I must strive to please him — and pray that someday I will bear him a son."

"Here, my lady," Rachel said. "There are bracelets here on this little stand. Did my lord give them to you? Did you forget to wear them?"

Abigail slipped the narrow bands over her hands and felt the cool metallic touch of the bracelets on her wrists.

"Yes, I forgot," she said, putting behind the childish rebellion that had made her leave the bracelets untouched on the stand.

Nabal was stretched out on a couch when she came into

the dining room. He looked up, hearing the jangle of the bracelets. Abigail met his look of pleased possessiveness with a smile.

"We'll hurry, my lord," she said.

He sat back with a sigh of pleasure.

He's nothing to be afraid of at all, Abigail thought with a sudden sort of revelation. *He's foolish and vain — perhaps even stupid — but I don't have to be afraid.*

Nabal has slain his thousands, she sang inside her head, *and Abigail has slain her tens of thousands.* She had to hurry from the room so that the giggle she was unable to suppress would not be heard by her husband, who sat pouring wine into a cup that had already been emptied at least once.

8

THE BURNING HEAT of midday held Eliab and Benjamin prisoners in the shade of a wide terebinth tree. Benjamin sat with his eyes closed against the shimmer of the light, but Eliab was restless, looking from side to side, squinting against the sun.

"I'm worried about Abigail," Eliab said, so suddenly that Benjamin gave a startled grunt. "The child she was expecting should have been born by now. We should have had word."

"Perhaps the child is late."

"Nevertheless, we should have had word. I have a feeling — I can't explain it — I have a feeling something is wrong."

"Would that donkey of a husband of hers tell us if something went wrong?" Benjamin asked.

"You're overly harsh in your judgment of the man. Just because he was — drunk when you were there —"

Benjamin interrupted. "I have been there twice — and not welcome either time. At least not by him. And both times I saw him drunk — and if not cruel to Abigail, at least not kind to her either."

"But you insisted, when you came home, that she was not really unhappy."

Benjamin sat up straighter, put his arms around his knees, and turned to face his father squarely. "She wasn't unhappy, but she was different. She was — hard, I think. She was no longer the honest girl I knew. She pretended to be a good wife, but out of his sight she followed her own counsel."

"She's his wife and she wanted to have a child. How else is a woman to act?"

"My mother has never needed to be two people," Benjamin muttered.

Eliab smiled at his son. "Your mother is much loved. See that your wife is loved as much when you marry."

Benjamin glanced at his father. "I've told you that I would settle for the little maid of Abigail's."

"Not a seemly thing — to take your sister's slave as wife."

"Why not? She's healthy and beautiful, and I'd wager her background is as good as ours. Nabal probably won her services in some deceitful way."

Eliab shook his head fretfully. "I have other things to worry about just now. I don't like it that we have not heard from Abigail. Her mother is fretting. I sometimes wonder if I should go myself to see if all is well."

"Let me go," Benjamin urged. "I can represent you, and I am younger and so the journey wouldn't be as hard on me."

Eliab hesitated. "You have a hot temper, my son. Your knuckles are still skinned from that skirmish with Joel when you found him mistreating the sheep. I'm not sure I could trust you to be courteous to Nabal."

Benjamin looked at his hands ruefully. "Old Joel is a brute," he argued, then added, "but I suppose I did react hastily. I'm sure I would be wiser with my own brother-in-law."

"And you could see the little Rachel," Eliab said dryly. "I doubt that your eagerness shows much concern for your sister."

Benjamin did not smile. "The only reason I have not begged you to get Rachel for me before now is because I'm so sure Abigail needs her. You think I'm not concerned for my sister? Well, you're wrong. I grieve for her, remembering the smallness of her and the courage and the laughter. Do you think it was easy for me, seeing her brittle and cool and almost old?"

Eliab sighed heavily. "But you've also said that she has bracelets on her arms, and that her dresses are embroidered with rich threads, and that the whole household obeys her."

"Well, those things are true, too," Benjamin admitted. "It's just that I — well, I wish things were different. I'm not sure, myself, how she could have conceived a child. Her husband is a drunken fool. I'm surprised he fulfilled his duties as a husband. No wonder it took her more than a year to conceive."

"Benjamin!" Eliab thundered. "I won't have such talk."

The boy didn't answer and lay back again, closing his eyes against the sky's glare.

After a long silence, Eliab spoke again, his voice quiet. "You're right about some things, though. And perhaps you *are* the one to go. It might not be very easy for me if things are as you say."

Benjamin's voice was steady. "I'll leave in the morning. I'll confess now that I've been uneasy, too. I was afraid you'd think I only wanted to go because of Rachel."

"Don't be gone too long," Eliab said. "Bring me word as soon as possible. I'm anxious."

"You're more than anxious," Benjamin announced, looking at his father. "You're afraid. We're both afraid."

The sound of professional mourners floated in a dark wave up to the room where Abigail lay. Nabal had hired them to wail and scratch themselves, even though the child had only lived four days. He had not asked Abigail's feelings on the subject. He had, in fact, not spoken to her at all. If he felt any compassion for the girl who had struggled in agony for two days to bring forth a puny, sickly man child, he had not shown it. He had gone coldly and methodically about the business of hiring the mourners, making burial arrangements, and calling in a priest. Then he had proceeded to get drunker than she had ever seen him, and he had not been sober since.

I should get up, Abigail thought. *I should join the mourners and weep for the child.* But she could not force herself to move.

She felt as though a great weight were pressing down on her body.

And yet, there was anger in her, too — a hot, blazing anger that burned in her throat until she gagged on it. Why had Yahweh allowed this thing to happen? Oh, yes, it was true that babies died, but why the child she had conceived with such difficulty? Why the child who could have brought joy and fulfillment into her life?

I prayed, Abigail thought, knotting her fists. *I prayed that all would be well with the child. I did nothing wrong. I was docile and obedient during the months that I carried him. I never went outside the compound. I never ran in the open field as I longed to do. I did everything I should. And in return, Yahweh has killed my child.*

Dry sobs racked her body. She remembered the feel and smell of the child, the weak tugging of his lips at her breast, the tiny fingers that had clutched so feebly at hers. As though the image were burned on her brain, she saw the small face, the fuzz of dark hair, the eyes that had been so astonishingly like her mother's.

And now he was dead. The son she had prayed for was dead.

"I can't stand it," Abigail said out loud. "Where were You, Yahweh, when the child was growing in my body? Where was the life and strength that You give to healthy babies? Why have You deserted me in this — this foreign place?" Holding her hands over her face, she wept despairingly.

"My lady." Rachel came softly, her voice a caress. "My lady, don't weep. I have something wonderful to tell you."

"Wonderful?" Abigail stared with dull apathy. "How can anything be wonderful?"

"Your brother is here," Rachel whispered. "Your brother has come."

"Benjamin?" Abigail gasped in astonishment. "Benjamin is *here*?"

"Here, my lady." Rachel's tear-swollen eyes gleamed brightly.

Abigail threw off the light cover that she had pulled over herself in spite of the heat of the day, and tried to get up from the mat. But her legs would not hold her, and she slumped against her pillows. "I can't get up," she moaned. "Bring him here. Oh, hurry, Rachel, bring him here."

"He's just outside the door, my lady. Here — see — here he is."

For a few seconds Benjamin stood, blinking in the dimness of his sister's sleeping room, and then quickly and clumsily, he moved toward her and knelt beside her on the floor. "I'm sorry," he said awkwardly. "I'm sorry about the baby."

"Oh, Benjamin!" She caught at him with trembling hands and pushed herself against the comfort of his chest. "Oh, Benjamin." Suddenly, remembering the Law, she pulled back. "I'm still unclean," she cried. "You'll be unclean from touching me."

"What does it matter?" he said. "I can cleanse myself at sunset."

He held her and stroked her hair, pressing his cheek against the top of her head. And, in his arms, she wept without restraint, feeling a gradual loosening of the anger and anguish that had been knotted so tightly in her heart. It was not that her grief was lessened; it was only that she felt it was no longer necessary for her to bear it all alone.

"How did you know?" she gasped at last. "How did you know to come?"

"I didn't hear about the baby until just now when I arrived and Rachel told me. But Father was worried — we were both worried. We had to know how things were with you."

"Oh, I'm so glad, so glad," she sobbed. "Oh, Benjamin, I've been dying of homesickness and pain. And there was no one."

"Surely Rachel?" he began.

She nodded vigorously against his shoulder. "Yes, of course. Rachel is wonderful. But she — she's not from home."

"Well, I'm here now," Benjamin said. "Lie back on the pillows and rest. You're so thin — come, lie back. I won't leave you."

Gently, he loosened her clinging fingers and laid her back against the pillow. "There," he said. "Is that better?"

"How are Mother and Father?" she asked, her words tripping on her sobs. "You'll have to tell them about the baby." Her eyes filled again.

"They're fine, just fine. Only worried about you, of course. And when I go home, I'll tell them about the baby — about everything. You're not to worry, you hear?"

A furious, slurred voice came suddenly from the doorway. "I heard there was a man in my wife's bedroom. What do you think you're doing up here?"

Benjamin turned to look at his brother-in-law. "Greetings, brother," he said, struggling to keep his voice civil. "Don't you recognize me? Surely you would not object to your wife's brother visiting her in her grief?"

Nabal was very drunk. His mouth was slack and foolish, and there was a glazed, unfocused look in his eyes.

"I want no man in this room. If my wife is incapable of bearing a healthy son for me, she is incapable of entertaining guests."

Abigail caught her breath in a sharp hiss of pain, and at the sound, Benjamin stood to face his brother-in-law.

"That was hardly fair, was it?" he asked quietly. "Her sorrow is surely as deep as your own. Why do you blame her for what is certainly not her fault?"

"How do you know what is her fault and what isn't?" Nabal shouted, holding the doorway for support. "For all you know, she deliberately failed to take care of herself while she carried the child."

Abigail pushed herself up onto her elbow. "You're drunk," she said coldly, bitterly.

None of them was prepared for Nabal's action. He had seemed too drunk to do more than lean against the wall. But before anyone realized what he intended to do, he was stooping over Abigail, and the loud smack of his hand across her face sounded over the distant wail of the mourners.

Benjamin stood for a few seconds in mute astonishment. He stared from Abigail's stony silence, as she huddled against the pillows, one palm cupping her cheek, to Rachel's blank look and stiffly held hands.

"That isn't the first time you've done that, is it?" Benjamin asked. "Both of these girls act as though they've been through this before."

Nabal staggered as he righted himself. "No woman is going to tell *me* I'm drunk."

Benjamin lunged at the man with silent fury. His first blow knocked Nabal to the floor. A second later, Benjamin had hauled the older man up with his left hand and had started a systematic slapping that knocked Nabal's face first to one side and then to the other.

Abigail fought to get to her feet, but although Rachel ran to help her, she could only crouch on her hands and knees, trying to call out to the struggling men.

"No," she gasped. "No, Benjamin, *please*. He'll have you killed. He will. Oh, Benjamin, *stop!*"

Benjamin acted as though he didn't hear her. With an awful rhythm, his hand slapped back and forth — hitting Nabal first with his smacking palm, then with the knuckle-cracking sound of the back of his hand.

"Hit her, will you?" Benjamin spit out. "Hit her while she's down with grief and pain. You — you pig!"

The ugly epithet was shot out with venom although it was obvious that Nabal did not hear what was being said.

"Stop," Abigail cried. "Benjamin, stop! Oh, Yahweh, stop him." She swayed weakly, horror etched on her face.

Her last cry seemed to reach Benjamin, and with one final swing of his hand, he dropped Nabal. The man fell to the floor with a thud.

"He's dead," Abigail moaned. "Benjamin, what have you done?"

Benjamin was gasping with shallow, rapid breaths. "He's

not dead. You're not that lucky. I've only knocked him senseless."

Abigail rocked back and forth on her knees in an agony of fear. "He'll kill you," she wept. "He has servants who are bigger than you and who will do anything at his bidding. I swear to you, Benjamin, he'll kill you."

"I don't think —" Benjamin began, but Rachel, holding onto her mistress, interrupted.

"She's right, my lord. You wouldn't be the first man who had angered him and died. Please, you mustn't stay here."

Benjamin looked from one girl to the other. Their obvious terror seemed to finally convince him. "I'll start back home," he muttered.

Abigail tried to bring stillness and clarity into her mind so that she could make some kind of intelligent plan. "No, not home," she cried. "He'd look there first. You'll have to hide somewhere. Isn't there any place you can think of that would be safe?"

Rachel's voice came with surprising authority. "There's the wilderness of Paran, my lady. I've told you that my brother is there with David. You'd be safe there, my lord," she said.

Benjamin's eyes lit up. "David? You mean David of Bethlehem?"

"Yes, my lord. He fled there when King Saul tried to kill him. Other men who are also outcasts have joined him."

Abigail felt a frenzy of fear rising in her. "Don't stand and talk. Can't you see that my husband might wake up at any moment?"

"But —" Benjamin began.

She cut in with a breathless sob. "Rachel will show you how to get down to the stables the back way. Take several of the horses for yourself and your servant. If anyone questions you, show them this ring and say you are sent on an errand. Please, please, don't wait another minute."

"But our parents — what will they think?"

"I'll try to get word to them. Just hurry!"

"I only wanted to help," Benjamin began, but before he could add anything, Nabal began to moan.

Abigail felt the blood drain from her face, and she lifted stricken eyes to her brother.

Benjamin stooped swiftly and lightly kissed her cheek. "Then I'll go," he murmured. "When it's safe for me to come back, will you send me word?"

"I promise," she said. "May Yahweh go with you!"

Benjamin's hand reached toward Rachel, and the two of them ran swiftly from the room. Nabal groaned and stirred again and then lay motionless. Until she heard the horses gallop from the yard, Abigail sat in rigid stillness. Then she turned to her husband.

She had thought she could not get up from her bed, but of course she could. She could do anything she had to do. She dipped a cloth in water and slowly, mechanically, began to wipe Nabal's battered face. At last he opened his eyes and looked at her in confusion.

"My lord," she said. "Don't try to move or talk. You're hurt. Let me hold you."

She gathered him up as she would gather up a hurt child, and he lay in her arms, weeping. She had thought she would never be able to touch him again, but she had reckoned without the mercy of Yahweh. Because, through the chaos of her anger and grief, she was suddenly filled with a cool, clear serenity. It was as though the fragile weight of Samuel's hands lay again on her head.

And I thought, because the baby died, that You had deserted me. Oh, Yahweh, my Lord, she thought. *Who else but you could give me the strength to hold this man and minister to him?*

Slowly, Nabal's eyes cleared as his memory returned. He lay very still, looking up at Abigail.

"He struck me," he mumbled. "Your brother struck me."

"Yes, my lord," she said meekly. "So I've sent him away. I've told him he is never to come back to the house of my lord."

Nabal stared at her for a long time, his face registering

both doubt and contempt, but he did not try to move away from her. *He may not believe me,* Abigail thought, *but at least I have purchased a little time for Benjamin.*

"Rest, my lord," she said gently. "Lie still and rest."

She held him until her arms felt as though they were nearly broken, and then Rachel, who had crept silently back into the room, helped her place him against the pillows. The girls were quiet, and until they were sure he slept, they did not even risk looking at each other lest Nabal guess their guilty secret.

9

THAT NIGHT, Abigail dreamed again that she was on the rooftop of her father's home in Hebron. Just as on the night when Samuel was a guest in the house, she dreamed that she crouched alone in the dark, windy corner and listened to her father and Samuel talking. And, as before, she could hear only the sound of their voices, not the words they spoke. Her father's voice was low and familiar and comforting, but Samuel's voice was as hollow as the sound of a reed that has been scraped out to make a shepherd's flute. She strained forward, but no amount of straining could break the sound of the voices into comprehensible words.

Then, just as before, she heard the single word, "David." It was said in the clear, strong voice of her father and repeated in the hollow voice of Samuel. And once more, the name blew across the roof and ran around the sky. But this time, instead of being whispered, the name echoed from the hills in wind and thunder. The whole earth and sky were vibrating with the sound of "David... David... David."

In her dream, Abigail heard the name with a fierce, sudden joy. She stood up from her hiding place to look fearlessly at her father and Samuel.

"David," she cried out in her sleep, and it was as though her grief over the child's death were miraculously eased by the saying of the name.

Her father smiled at her, but when Samuel turned his head to look at her, she saw his face dissolved into nothingness.

"My lord," she cried, running to cast herself at his feet. "My lord, bless me again."

When she looked up, Samuel was gone, and her father was sitting alone on the dark, windy rooftop, his face wet with tears.

"My lady. My lady, wake up." Rachel's hand was firm and real on Abigail's shoulder. "You're dreaming. Don't be afraid. Everything will be all right."

Abigail came slowly awake. "Samuel," she mumbled. "I was dreaming of the high priest, Samuel. And of my father." Even to Rachel, she could not talk of the joy that had filled her at the sound of David's name.

"Yes, my lady. Try to sleep again. It's not dawn yet."

Soothed by Rachel's voice and hand, Abigail obediently turned on her side. She was almost asleep when a dark certainty caught and held her. *Samuel,* she thought. *He's dead.* She lay very still, letting herself remember the hollow sound of his voice in her dream, the way his face had dissolved into nothingness.

Samuel's dead, she thought bleakly. *I've lost my baby, and now Samuel is dead.* She wept quietly, patiently, as with an old sorrow while Rachel sat beside her, smoothing back her hair.

The next morning, Abigail learned that Nabal had ridden, with his men, to Hebron. He left word that he had gone to tell Abigail's parents of the death of the child, but she knew that his real purpose was to try to find Benjamin. She felt a deep sense of gratitude that Rachel had known of the sanctuary in the wilderness of Paran. Her only concern now was that she was unable to tell her parents where Benjamin was.

Nabal was gone six days. When he returned, he was sober, cool, and reserved.

"Your parents are well," he said to Abigail. "They're grieved about the child, of course. But they're well, except for being worried about their son. He has never come home — and I could offer them no comfort, of course."

"Of course not," she murmured. Then, gathering up her courage, she said, "Do you suppose I could go to Hebron to visit them, my lord? When I'm well enough to travel, I mean."

He smiled benignly, as though to grant her desires were his only wish in life. "Perhaps," he said. "Perhaps you could go in a month or so and be back in plenty of time to help with the shearing celebration. Does that seem sensible to you?"

She looked at him warily. There seemed to be no deception in him, and the thought crossed her mind that if he were like this all the time, she could be a good and dutiful wife. She might never love him; she could, if things were different, respect him.

"Yes, my lord. Sensible and very generous of you. I would really like to go to Hebron, my lord. It has been more than two years since I've seen my parents."

"Well, perhaps," he said again. "If you don't offend me, of course." His voice was smooth as oil, his smile almost sincere. "Oh, by the way, the high priest of Israel died. I think you spoke of meeting him once. Samuel. I heard the news in Hebron. He lies in Ramah, I was told, where he's being mourned by his followers."

She stood rooted, not really shocked. "Died?" she whispered. "When?"

"Several nights ago. I'm not sure when. At least King Saul can do as he pleases now, without Samuel's constant harping and criticism."

"But Samuel was Yahweh's spokesman," she dared to say.

Nabal shrugged. "Samuel was a fanatical old man. I don't know why Saul ever listened to him in the first place."

She opened her mouth to answer, but Nabal said sharply, "I've said all I want to say. I don't want to hear any sentimental drivel from a silly woman."

Her anger did not even show in her eyes. "Yes, my lord," she said meekly. "Would my lord care for something to eat or drink? May I serve him?"

Nabal smiled with satisfaction. His fingers lightly touched the bruises under his eyes, as though to remind himself of the need for her submission. "Just some wine and fruit. I'm not really hungry. Bring plenty of wine."

"Yes, my lord," she whispered. Slipping from the room, she gave quick orders to the women in the kitchen. While she waited for them to bring the wine and a basket of fruit, she stood rigid, forcing herself to accept the truth of Samuel's death. In her heart, she had known it, of course, but the confirmation of it was still painful.

I wish I could go to Ramah, she mourned. *I wish I could kneel beside him and touch his feet and weep for him so that everyone could see my grief.*

Looking up, she saw a servant approaching with the wine. "Here," Abigail said, "give it to me. I'll serve my lord."

A thought blazed through her mind in the instant before she entered the room where Nabal sat. David would surely go to Ramah. David would kneel beside the old prophet in spite of the threat of Saul. David would touch his feet, Abigail thought, and oddly enough, she was comforted by that. If she could not go to Ramah herself, then there was solace in the thought that David would be there.

Her few days at home were like a green oasis in a desert land. To her astonishment, Nabal had really let her travel back to Hebron, and the joy of seeing her parents had been even greater than she had anticipated. The feel of their arms around her, the sound of their voices, and the serenity of the house that held love and happiness within its walls were like cool water to a thirsty traveler.

She spent hours with her father in the field, sitting beside him, absorbing his words and his nearness. After telling him the truth about Benjamin and something of the death of the child, she did not refer again to life in her husband's house. Nothing was going to change the fact that although she was only seventeen, she was not a child in any way. She was a woman and Nabal's wife until he died or divorced her. It was better, by far, to talk of other things.

So she and her father discussed the sheep and the need for rain. They spoke of Benjamin's living with David's army — "Truly an army?" she had asked in amazement when her father used the word — in the wilderness of Paran. Sometimes, they sat quietly together and watched the shadows drift across the land, each one content with the silence of the other.

But some days, Abigail stayed with her mother. She had an entirely different attitude toward Zopporah now, Abigail realized. Where once she had been impatient and even critical of her mother, now she turned to the older woman for help.

"How did you bear it?" Abigail asked one afternoon. "When your babies died? You lost four of them. How did you bear it?"

Zopporah smiled at her daughter, but her lips trembled when she spoke. "Without Yahweh, and your father, I would have died."

"Yahweh?" True, her mother had talked a great deal about Yahweh's rules for women and the need to be obedient to Him, but the girl had never been aware of more than that. One did not think of someone like plump, gentle Zopporah when one thought of complete dependence on Yahweh. One thought of Samuel, who had heard the voice of God. "Truly, Mother? You felt that close to Yahweh?"

Zopporah smoothed the folds of her robe over her lap. "You sound surprised. Just because I didn't talk about my faith doesn't mean I didn't have any."

Abigail was embarrassed. "I didn't mean *that*. Not really. I just — just meant that I thought you looked to Yahweh for laws, not for comfort."

"There's comfort in laws," Zopporah said confidently.

"Laws give shape to life. Without them, life becomes only a tangle of conflicting wills."

Abigail nodded thoughtfully. "Yes, I see that. But, Mother, tell me more about your dependence on Yahweh. Tell me what you *did* when your heart was broken."

Zopporah's eyes blurred with remembering. "Like you," she said softly, "I was the child of a godly father. He taught me the words of the Law. Perhaps also like you, I had memorized the words without knowing what they meant. But in my hours of anguish, I remembered. I used to say the words over and over to myself. Especially these: 'And I will have regard for you and make you fruitful and multiply you, and will confirm my convenant with you. And I will make my abode among you and my soul shall not abhor you. ... And I will walk among you, and I will be your God, and you shall be my people.' It seemed very clear to me," she finished simply.

Abigail stared at her mother. Of course, she had heard the words many times before. They were as familiar as the sound of her own breathing. But, said in her mother's voice in this moment of sharing a mutual pain, the words vibrated with new meaning.

"It's a promise, isn't it?" Abigail asked slowly. "Yahweh wouldn't make a promise He had no intention of keeping, would He?"

"I never thought so," Zopporah replied.

They were quiet. "And do you think," Abigail said at last, shaping the words carefully, "that Yahweh's promise would have been enough if my father had been — less of a comfort than he was?"

Zopporah's eyes moved away from her daughter's face. She swallowed several times before she finally spoke. "I think so, yes. There may come a time when I no longer have your father to comfort me. Then I will have to depend entirely on Yahweh to give me the courage to live. Just as He will give you courage when the next child is born."

"*If* there is another child," Abigail said. "It took me more than a year to conceive the first one."

"Yahweh's ways are not always easy to understand," Zopporah admitted. "But His mercy is unfailing."

For the first time since the baby died, Abigail felt the faint swelling of hope where there had been only despair.

The day before she was to return to Nabal's house, Abigail sat alone in the yard. Rachel was busy packing things for the return journey, and Zopporah was in the kitchen, making the small honey cakes that Abigail loved. Eliab had gone to the fields early so that he might return early in order to greet the relatives and friends who were coming for the evening meal to celebrate Abigail's last day at home.

She was surprised to see Eliab, accompanied by a stranger, come suddenly around the corner. He had not planned to come this soon.

"Daughter," Eliab called. "Come and help me make our guest welcome. He has traveled a long way, and he's tired and thirsty."

Abigail, surprised that her father had called to her instead of to one of the servants, hastily filled a pitcher from the water jar and carried it to the gate.

The stranger, tall and dark-skinned, smiled gratefully as she poured out a cup of water for drinking and then splashed clean water in the basin that stood at the gate for the washing of feet.

"This is my daughter, the wife of Nabal of Maon," Eliab said. "Abigail, this is Ethan. He comes from the wilderness of Paran."

Abigail felt a quick rush of excitement. "You bring news of my brother?" she cried.

"Later," Eliab said. He cast a quick warning glance toward Nabal's men who had served as a bodyguard for Abigail and Rachel and who were now gathered in the far corner of the yard. "Tell your mother we have another guest for dinner."

She had to be content with that, but the sparkle in the stranger's eyes held the promise of happy news.

The evening passed in a swirl of laughter, good food, and warm conversation, but finally the guests were gone and

Ethan, who was on his way to Bethlehem to get word of David's parents, could begin to give the news his hosts were eager to hear.

"Your son has won David's trust already," Ethan said with pride. "The lad is a natural soldier and will soon be captain of one of the troops. At the present time, he rides out against the outlaws that harass the southern border of Judah."

"Is he in danger then?" Zopporah asked, casting a quick look at her husband as if to apologize for the question.

Ethan laughed. "Not really. At least not much. David's men seem to lead charmed lives. Every man who follows David believes that Yahweh has set His mark on him."

"Even with Saul still king?" Eliab asked.

Ethan sent a level look at his host. "David is loyal to Saul, sir. He has given us orders again and again to spare the life of Saul and Jonathan if we should ever meet them in battle."

Eliab sighed with relief. "That's good. The thought of rebellion against Yahweh's anointed is terrible to me. Oh, I know, I know. I know how David has been treated, and I know that Samuel loved David and chose him for the next king. But can I help it if my heart hopes that the transition will come without additional fighting among the people of Yahweh?"

"You think as David does," Ethan said. "There will be no shifting him, I promise you. In the meantime, we see that our fellow tribesmen from Judah can pasture their sheep safely without being attacked by desert nomads." He looked at Abigail. "Your lord Nabal would be grateful to us if he knew how often we've stopped raids on those herds of his that are pastured out toward the wilderness."

She smiled. "I doubt that my lord would acknowledge David's help. Especially if he knew that Benjamin is one of David's followers."

Ethan grinned back at her. "That's exactly what Benjamin said. He's been worried about you. Are you all right?"

"Tell him I'm fine. Tell him I've learned to be submissive at last. Or I am most of the time. Tell him not to worry."

"He's been trying to come up with a plan that would let him come to Nabal's house to see you."

"No!" Abigail's voice was sharp. "No, he must not. Not yet. My lord Nabal is not ready yet to see Benjamin. Tell him I'll get word to him when the time is right."

Eliab grinned at his guest with a faint touch of embarrassment. "She's very strong-minded, this daughter of mine."

Ethan's face held only admiration. "I'm looking forward to seeing her again," he admitted. "I'm sure that Nabal will be approached by David's men soon. It's our custom to ask for food and supplies from men whose shepherds and herds we've protected. Most men are willing to pay the price, even when the request comes as a surprise."

Abigail shook her head. "You don't know my lord Nabal. He can be very generous, if he wants, but he can be very formidable as well. Must you come to Nabal's house?"

"He's one of the wealthiest landowners," Ethan said. "We've spent a great deal of time and energy looking out for his shepherds and his sheep. It's only fair that he pay us for our pains."

"Then," Abigail said, "I can only hope that my lord will be receptive to the request of David when it comes." She turned to her parents. "I have a very long ride tomorrow and I need to rest. Will you excuse me?"

Zopporah got up to follow her daughter. "I'll come, too," she said.

Abigail saw the sadness in her mother's eyes, but at first said nothing. What comfort could she offer when nothing could be done to prevent the fact that Abigail had to go back to Nabal and leave her mother alone again? And this time it would be worse because Benjamin was gone, too.

They walked up the shadowy steps together, their small lamps making flickering splotches of light on the walls and on their faces. At the top of the steps, Abigail stopped to lay her hand along her mother's cheek. "I'm just sorry you have to be alone," Abigail said, unable to think of better words. Zopporah didn't answer, but Abigail saw the negative shake of her mother's head. "But you're not lonely, are you?" Abigail asked, her voice wistful. "You have Yahweh with you — *truly* with you. Pray for me, Mother, that I may have the same comfort when I'm away from my father's house."

part II

And it came about as she was riding on her donkey... that behold, David and his men were coming down toward her; so she met them.... So David received from her hand what she had brought him, and he said to her, "Go up to your house in peace."... But... in the morning, when the wine had gone out of Nabal,... his wife told him these things, and his heart died within him so that he became as a stone.... and he died.... Then David sent a proposal to Abigail, to take her as his wife.

1 Samuel 25:20, 35, 37-38, 39b

10

THE FIRE WAS CAREFULLY BANKED so that neither fuel would be wasted nor excess light spilled out across the night to inform desert wanderers that men lived here where caves fissured the stony hillside. Between fire and caves, a dozen men sat on the hard ground.

"And my parents are reconciled to the idea of being in Moab, then?" The question was asked with intensity. "None of the family has heard that they are unhappy?"

"My lord, as near as I could determine, your parents are more than reconciled. They're really happy to do anything for you."

"Thank you, Ethan. I've been worried about them. In Moab, they're safe from Saul's anger. Your journey to Bethlehem was worthwhile, if for no other reason than the fact that my heart is easier now. Do you have anything else to report?"

The firelight heightened the beauty of the speaker. His eyes reflected the gold of the flame, and his face and hair were touched with a warm glow.

"If David will permit me," Ethan said, "I have news for Benjamin."

David's wave toward Benjamin was a sign of gracious consent. Ethan leaned toward the young Calebite who sat closer to David than his length of time with the band would seem to warrant. Benjamin, too, leaned forward eagerly. "You saw my parents in Hebron?" he asked. "They seem well?"

"I saw your parents indeed," Ethan said with a smile. "I ate with them at a very festive meal. They were celebrating your sister's last evening at home before she returned to her husband."

"Abigail? You saw Abigail?" Benjamin's voice was astonished and excited. "Her husband let her go to Hebron? How was she? Has she recovered from the loss of the child?"

David laughed, and several of the men joined him. "You seem more concerned about your sister than about your parents," David said. "You're sure this *is* a sister you're talking about — not a cousin who has captured your heart?"

Benjamin grinned. "Only a sister, my lord. But I've told you about her. She's the one whose husband mistreated her in her grief, so that I attacked him. She's the reason I came here when I did."

David nodded. "Oh, yes, I remember. The girl who's married to Nabal, am I right?"

"Yes, my lord. Nabal, the wealthiest herder around here. We protect his sheep and shepherds as much as any."

"And has he paid his fee of gratitude?" David asked, looking over toward another of the men.

The man grinned at his master's choice of words. "No, my lord. According to my records, he's next on the list. My spies have told me that Nabal will be holding the shearing festival this week. It would be a good time to confront him, my lord. Plenty of food and everyone in a good mood."

Benjamin made a rueful sound, and David swung his head back around to look at him. "You don't sound hopeful. You haven't much regard for Nabal, I know, but surely you don't think he'd be foolish enough to ignore our request?"

"It would depend a great deal on whether or not he's sober," Benjamin replied. "The man is drunk a great deal of the time."

"And yet your parents gave your sister to him?"

Benjamin met his leader's incredulous look with some embarrassment. "We didn't know the man's failings until after she was betrothed, my lord."

David shrugged. "Then your sister has a hard time of it."

"She's very small, my lord, and prettier than sisters usually are. And she's married to a fool!"

"Let's hope the man is not foolish enough to turn down our request when our men go up to see him. I wouldn't like to have to kill off your tribesman, Benjamin."

Benjamin grinned. "Just as long as you spare my sister, my lord."

"Bloodthirsty, isn't he?" David said to the others. His glance came back to Benjamin. "Perhaps your sister will speak for us?"

"If her husband will listen," Benjamin muttered.

The talk died down and the men went, one by one, into the caves to stretch out on their cloaks, which they laid over rough pallets on the ground.

At last, David sat alone by the fire. His eyes were fastened on the black skies, starred with silver. For a few minutes he could forget the planning and the hiding, the fighting and the loneliness. He could forget the days in the house of a king, the marriage to a king's daughter, the friendship of a king's son. He could sit in utter stillness and look on the work of Yahweh's hands.

"The heavens declare the glory of God," he whispered.

The blurred fragment of a tune came and went in his mind. But the words were good and firm in his head. Someday he would make a song that started with those words. Someday when he was not so lonely and not pursued by a mad king.

But for now, he had other things to think about. There was, for example, the task of choosing the right men to go to see Nabal. Too bad he couldn't send Benjamin, but that would be dangerous. Well, there was Ethan. Perhaps Ethan could say the words that would move Nabal to be generous.

The sheep-shearing celebration had been going on for several days, and already at noon of the third day, Nabal's house was filled with laughter and music and the good smells of cooking food. Abigail, trying to be everywhere at once, was beginning to feel the heaviness of fatigue. Well, there were only two more days, and then the great throng of men who had come to help Nabal's shepherds shear the thousands of sheep would be gone. In the meantime, there was nothing to do but smile at her toiling servants, encourage them with words or actual help, and try to ignore the fact that her husband had not been wholly sober since the first evening of the celebration.

"Do you think our lord will want to serve the date wine tonight?" one of the kitchen servants asked. "Or should we wait until the last night to serve it?"

There was a tart rejoinder on Abigail's tongue. She wanted to say, "Why don't you ask *him*? Or is he too drunk to listen?" But, of course, she didn't say it. She had schooled herself to keep a smiling face and to make her voice sound unruffled and calm.

"If the date wine is very good," she said, "why not serve it tonight? By the last day, most of the men will be so relieved that the work is over that they'll hardly notice what they're drinking. We can use some of the thinner wine then."

"Yes, my lady." The girl bobbed her head and scuttled toward the kitchen. She had not indicated by word or look that she, too, was aware of Nabal's drunkenness. But Abigail knew she was. All the servants were aware. The men who rode with him thought their master's drinking only amusing, but Abigail had caught looks of scorn or disgust on the faces of the other servants. Although Abigail knew the dangers of a servant's scorn, there was little she could do about it except to concentrate, as she had done since she had become mistress of the house, on earning the respect and loyalty of the servants. Since she never showed her own contempt for her husband, except occasionally to Rachel, she continued to hope for a show of faithfulness from the household.

There was the sudden sound of voices raised in anger, and she looked quickly into the room where the shearers were eating to see if a fight had started. To her amazement, it was Nabal who was shouting at a group of young men who were standing around his chair. She watched for a second, but since the men had their backs to her and none of them looked familiar, she merely shrugged and turned away. It was surely no concern of hers.

The men Abigail had seen ringed Nabal in with hostility and anger. But the host of the house merely lounged back in his chair and laughed up into their flushed faces.

"So you're followers of David, are you?" he sneered, the words slurring together. "And who is this David? The son of Jesse, you say. What is that to me?"

"I assure you, my lord," Ethan said, holding his voice calm with an effort. "I assure you that David is a man of power and strength. It will not be wise to anger him. Give him the food he requests, my lord. All of your neighbors have done so."

Nabal laughed again. "My neighbors are fools if they submit to this kind of blackmail. I have no intentions of catering to some low-born desert outlaw."

"My lord," Ethan said urgently, "I advise you —"

Nabal jerked forward in his chair. The sudden movement made him wince a little and lift his hand gingerly to his forehead. "You're beginning to annoy me," he said. "But— wait! I'm feeling generous today. Suppose I tell my servants —" His tongue stumbled over the sibilant word and he giggled foolishly before he tried again. "I'll tell my servants to fix you up a nice little basket. A loaf of bread, perhaps, and a handful of grapes. How would that be?"

The veins stood out along the sides of Ethan's neck. "My lord," he said, "there are six hundred followers of David. Your suggestion is an insult!"

Nabal jutted out his jaw. "Then be insulted," he said as clearly as he could, taking pains to shape the words carefully. "Go tell your outlaw friend that he can eat sand for all Nabal of Maon cares."

One of the men stepped forward, but Ethan's hand stopped him. Ethan bowed before Nabal with exaggerated courtesy. "I'll tell David you said so, my lord," he purred. "I'm sure he will respond personally. You may very well be sorry, my lord."

Nabal laughed scornfully. "Your threats do not frighten me," he said. "Now get out."

He lifted his wine glass and emptied it with a flourish and did not even watch the followers of David as they strode from the room.

Several hours later, worn out from the long hours of work, Abigail climbed the steps to her room. From the sounds in the dining room, there would be little shearing done during the afternoon. The men seemed far more interested in shouting out their bawdy songs and lying in the shade, and Nabal was in no condition to reprimand them. Fortunately, the work had begun very early in the morning and the men had worked willingly enough until noon, when they had gathered for eating.

She settled herself in a corner of the room where a wedge of shadow kept the whitewashed walls relatively cool. She leaned her head back against the wall and closed her eyes. For a few minutes, at least, she would sit quietly and rest before she faced the task of directing the work for the evening meal, which would, apparently, be only a continuation of the midday dinner.

"My lady." Rachel, weary and hot, stood in the doorway. "I hate to bother you, but one of the shepherds says he has to speak to you."

Abigail looked up in surprise. "One of the shepherds? What could he possibly have to say to me?"

Rachel looked worried. "He insisted, my lady. I think you had better see him. I'm afraid something's wrong."

Abigail sighed deeply. Probably some silly quarrel between two of the shearers that Nabal was too incoherent to resolve.

"All right," she said. "I'll be right down. Stay close by, will you? If his complaint doesn't take too long, I'd like you to help me bathe and change my clothes. No, I won't say 'if' — get the water ready. I'll *take* the time."

"Yes, my lady." Rachel smiled, probably happy to be called out of the kitchen, and ran for water.

Abigail pushed her hair back from her face and walked quickly to the foot of the steps and out into the kitchen area. A young man, obviously ill at ease, stood waiting near the wall.

"You're the one who asked to see me?" she asked.

"Yes, my lady. I'm sorry to bother you, but — it's a matter of life or death, my lady."

She raised her eyebrows. "Life or death? Aren't you being a little dramatic? Or has one of the shearers threatened to use his shearing knife on you?"

The man's eyes were steady. "No, my lady. It's your husband who's in danger. Perhaps even you, my lady."

Her voice was incredulous. "Nabal in danger? What do you mean?"

"Have you heard of David, the Bethlehemite, my lady? The one who lives in the wilderness of Paran?"

She felt the familiar kick over her heart. How could she have been so stupid as to have forgotten Ethan's promise to come to Nabal to ask for food? Why hadn't she known, as soon as she saw the young men clustered about Nabal, who they were?

"David?" she whispered. "Those men were from David?"

The shepherd looked relieved. "Then you *do* know, my lady. Listen. Here's what happened."

When he finished talking, Abigail stared at him. "And what did David's men do?" she asked.

"They left. They didn't say a word to anyone. They just turned and left."

She started to draw a breath of relief when the shepherd interrupted. "That doesn't mean what you think it does, my lady. They were angry. They were going back to tell David. One of them said as much to me."

"And what will David do?" she asked.

"He'll attack this place. No doubt about it. He's a good protector of all men of Judah until they cross him. Then he's their enemy. I think he'll come with the sword, my lady."

She put her hands up to her cheeks and stared at the man with horror. "What can we do?" she whispered.

"I don't know, my lady. I was hoping you'd think of something."

"Yes. Well, I'll try to think of something. Thank you for coming to me."

"It's nothing, my lady. I did it as much for me as you. I'm a part of this household, too, you know. And when David takes up his sword, there aren't many left alive."

He turned with a look over his shoulder and moved toward the room of laughing men. She saw the attempt at bravado with which he picked up a cup of wine, but she had also seen the whites of his eyes when he turned away. The man was terrified.

And so am I, Abigail thought. *I had believed there could be only joy at the sound of David's name. I had not known there could be terror as well. What will I do? Oh, what will I do?*

Almost without thought, she moved away from the sound of the celebration and finally found herself out by the rear wall, away from the house. It was quieter there, and she forced herself to be still so that she could consider the problem.

I wish my father were here, she thought. *I wish* — and then her panic-filled mind steadied and stilled itself. Her father's God was here; hadn't her mother promised as much?

What should I do? she cried out in silence. *Yahweh, Lord, show me what to do.*

As the stillness in the center of her being grew and spread, Abigail felt her mind working with clarity and speed. If David wanted and needed food, she would get it for him. There were servants she could trust who would be willing to bring food to her. And as for how David would get it, she, herself, would take it to him.

If she hurried, if the servants did exactly as she told them, she could get far down the valley so that she could meet David's men before they could get near Nabal's house. It was risky, of course, even though Nabal seemed fully occupied with the food and wine and laughter in the dining room. But she would have to hurry.

Looking up, she saw Rachel coming toward her. "What is it, my lady?" she called. "Are you all right? I have the water ready and your crimson robe — your best one. Can you come?"

"Yes," she said. "Just a minute. Run — quickly — and get Jared. I can trust him, can't I, Rachel?"

"Completely, my lady. But what —"

"Don't ask questions. Run!"

Almost immediately, the boy Jared was in front of Abigail. Without wasting words, she explained what had happened.

"And there's no use trying to reason with our lord," Jared said. "He's too foolish —" He clapped his hand over his mouth. "I'm sorry, my lady."

"We haven't time for that," she said. "Just do as I say. And do it without letting Nabal or his men see you. If you bring donkeys here, behind the trees, I think you can manage. Load them as quickly as you can. Use whatever means you need. I want you to bring two hundred loaves of bread and at least two jugs of wine. I know there are five sheep, roasted, which haven't been cut into yet. Load those. And bring five measures of roasted grain. And fruit. Pack a hundred clusters of raisins and two hundred cakes of figs. I know it seems like a great deal — but —"

"It's no more than David's men deserve, my lady," the boy cried. "My father's a shepherd and I know."

"But how will David get all this, my lady?" Rachel asked.

"I'm going to take it," Abigail said resolutely. "Jared, get several other men to accompany us — men I can trust. And hurry." She turned to Rachel. "Come now, we'll go to my room. I want to be bathed and dressed — in as fine a fashion as you know."

Rachel only nodded, and they ran together across the dusty yard toward the house.

11

THE DONKEY REINS were rough in Abigail's clenched hands, and for some time after they left Nabal's house, she saw nothing but the back of Jared, who rode directly in front of her, and heard nothing but the pounding of her own heart. Gradually, her feeling of panic subsided and she began to shape the words in her mind that she must say to David.

Say to David! A sudden stillness filled her. After the years of hearing about the young Bethlehemite and always with the shock of recognition that quickened her heart, she was finally going to meet him face to face. What *could* she say to him? Would she even be able to speak, or would her tongue cleave to the roof of her mouth so that she would be as one struck dumb?

No, surely Yahweh would not have spoken to her so clearly in the yard if He intended her to come before David voiceless. She thought of the story of Moses and his insistence that he could not speak for the Lord, so the Lord had provided Aaron for him. *Well, I have no Aaron,* Abigail thought, *so the Lord will simply have to loosen my tongue and give me the words.*

At first, she fumbled futilely for an explanation of why it was she who was coming to meet David, but gradually, with a feeling of warmth, words began to shape themselves in her mind. It was like making a song except that there was no tune to worry about. The making of a song had always seemed a magic thing to her — words fitting themselves together smoothly and sweetly. She had always known that it was Yahweh who gave her the songs she created. It was surely Yahweh, then, who formed the arguments and truths that went surging through her head.

Jared turned to his mistress. "Listen, my lady, listen. I hear mules coming. There, behind that slope of the hill, still hidden from us, but close."

She lifted her head and listened. The boy was right, and from the sound, there were many men coming.

"Let me ride ahead," she commanded with so resolute a voice that the boy drew in his beast and dropped behind her without even an argument.

If I'm wrong about this, Abigail thought, *if David's anger cannot be halted, then at least I will die by his hand.*

At that moment, the army from the wilderness came plunging around the curve of the hill, and she found herself staring into the faces of hundreds of men. For one second, she thought she might fall from her donkey, but almost instantly, she was filled with strength. She pulled hard on the reins, and when her donkey stopped, she slipped from its back to the ground and stood, waiting for David and his men.

The strong desert wind pulled her scarlet robe close to her body and whipped her head scarf out behind her. She felt her long hair tearing itself loose and flowing out with the filmy scarf. She was intensely, surprisingly aware of the flash of her gold bracelets in the sun, and she had a brief and comforting memory of the look of satisfaction on Rachel's face after she had applied kohl to her mistress's eyelids and darkened her lips with ointment. Abigail knew a quick gratitude that Yahweh had seen fit to make her beautiful. That, alone, might make David pause until she had said part of what she had to say.

She did not have to be told which of the approaching men

was David. Her heart recognized him instantly. She allowed herself one brief look at his bright hair and ruddy face before she dropped to her knees and bowed her face to the ground.

She could hear mules sliding to a stop.

"What's this?" David said, and his voice was filled with fury.

"It's Abigail, my lord. The wife of Nabal." She had heard him talking only once, but Abigail immediately recognized Ethan's voice.

"The wife of Nabal? The sister of Benjamin?"

She heard the sounds of several men dismounting, but she dared not look up.

"On me alone, my lord, be the blame," she said clearly. "Please, my lord, will you let your maidservant speak to you? Will you listen, my lord, to what she has to say?"

"How can I listen to you with your face in the sand?"

At that, she dared to lift her head. David was standing close to her, staring at her more with astonishment than annoyance.

"Did your lord send you?" he snapped.

"No. He doesn't know I'm here." She sat back on her heels, and David reached down to take her hand and raise her to her feet.

"Then Nabal's attitude hasn't changed?"

"Please, my lord, don't pay any attention to that worthless man." Her voice was sturdy even though she knew she had no right to say such things about her own husband. "He's rightly named, my lord. Nabal means 'a fool,' and that's exactly what he is."

David was silent, but he never took his eyes from her face.

"I didn't see your men, my lord, when you sent them to my husband's house. If I had —"

David interrupted abruptly. "I'm aware of that. Ethan said he looked for you but you weren't around."

"So you see, my lord —"

Once more, his voice snapped out. "What difference

does it make? The insult has been given and the punishment will be meted out."

"Oh, my lord, hear me. You haven't shed blood yet. You're still innocent of avenging yourself by your own hand. So — please let this food that I've brought be an apology that will stop my lord's anger."

David glanced away from her to look at the heavily burdened donkeys behind her. His eyes came back to her face, and it seemed to her that there was less anger in them.

"Please forgive me, my lord, if I have intruded, but I believe that Yahweh sent me to you."

"Yahweh?" His eyebrows went up, but there was the slightest softening of his lips, almost as though he wanted to smile but would not.

"Yes, my lord. I know that you're fighting the battles of Yahweh, my lord, and that He will give an enduring house to my lord, and evil shall not be found in you all your days."

The last words came out with an intimacy she had not planned.

But David was not offended. "And who told you all of this?" he asked, "Your brother?"

"Oh, no, my lord." She did not even look toward the mounted men to see if Benjamin were among them. "Samuel told me about you years ago. When he first anointed you in Bethlehem. And I — I have dreamed about you, my lord."

"Dreamed?"

"Yes, my lord. It was as though the earth and the sky — the very stars — were singing the name of David. I believe that Yahweh spoke to me through the dream. I think He said that if anyone should pursue you and try to take your life —" once more the words had slipped into intimate speech, and she hastily corrected herself. "If anyone should seek the life of my lord, then his life should be bound up in the bundle of the living with the Lord your God; but the lives of your enemies He shall sling out as from the hollow of a sling."

These were not the words she had planned. These words

were delivered into her mouth miraculously. She continued to look fearlessly into David's eyes as she went on speaking.

"And it shall come about when Yahweh has done to my lord all the good that has been promised that He shall appoint you ruler over Israel!"

David's breath was drawn in with a startled hiss.

Abigail spoke more softly so that it was almost as though there were only the two of them there. "And my lord will be grateful when that time comes that he has not avenged himself. Yahweh has said clearly that vengeance is His and His alone. Surely my lord knows that, and when he is ruler, he will be grateful that he has not shed blood without cause."

She stopped, feeling drained and hollow. Dropping her eyes from David's, she said shakily, "When Yahweh shall deal well with my lord, then remember your maidservant."

David slowly took her hands in his. His voice was husky when he said, "Blessed be the Lord God of Israel, who sent you this day to meet me."

She raised startled eyes to his, unprepared for his reaction.

"And blessed be your discernment," David went on gently, "and blessed be you who have kept me this day from bloodshed and from avenging myself with my own hand."

"Thank you, my lord," she whispered.

David let out his breath. "If you hadn't come — if Yahweh hadn't sent you, there's no question but what I would have killed every man of Nabal's — starting with Nabal himself."

She felt the unexpected sting of tears, thinking of the young servants, of the old shepherds who might even now be lying in a welter of blood. It was not until much later that she realized she had not even thought of Nabal.

"But come, my lord," she managed to say. "Here is food — take it as a gift from my hand."

"The sight of you is almost gift enough," David said, but in so soft a voice she knew no one else could hear. She realized, then, that he was still holding her hands, and she felt the blood run up her throat and face.

David smiled and released her hands reluctantly. He turned to his men. "Accept the lady's gift," he said. "And send word along the line to Benjamin that his sister is here and should like to talk to him."

"Oh, thank you, my lord," she cried. "I hadn't — hadn't even thought of Benjamin."

"I know," he said, and it was as though he had touched her.

She felt her heart race and turned with relief to the sight of Benjamin flinging himself from his mule.

"Abigail," he yelled, and rushed up to grab her in his arms.

"Oh, Benjamin," she cried, and could not tell, for a minute, if she were laughing or crying.

While the men unloaded the donkeys, Benjamin and Abigail stood and talked eagerly, trying to squeeze in everything they wanted to say.

"How's Rachel?" Benjamin asked at last. "Why didn't she come with you?"

"I left her at home to cover up for me in case my husband demanded my presence. She's fine." Abigail looked sharply at her brother. "Why do you ask? Or have I been blind that I hadn't noticed before this *why* you would ask."

Benjamin grinned. "I don't suppose one woman ever notices how lovely another one is."

"I notice everything about her," Abigail said soberly. "Oh, Benjamin, do you want her?"

"In time," Benjamin said. "When you don't need her so much. When life is better for me. But keep her safe for me."

Abigail smiled, but she could not repress the sudden thought that this was only one more way in which Nabal stood between her family and joy.

"I must go back," she said breathlessly to Benjamin. "If we're gone too long, it's sure to be noticed. Will you tell your leader — David — that I will be forever grateful for his kindness in listening to me?"

"You might tell him yourself." The voice came abruptly at her shoulder, and she turned to find herself face to face with the young Bethlehemite. He was smiling, and she felt almost dizzy looking at him. He was the most beautiful young man she had ever seen, she thought, and his eyes drew hers like a magnet. No wonder the men followed him and loved him.

For the first time since she had come, she smiled freely, and she saw his eyes brighten. "Thank you, my lord. I will truly be forever grateful."

"And I to you," he said. "Go to your house in peace." He lifted his hand as though to touch her and then let it drop. "Help her mount her beast," he said to Benjamin, "and send her safely on her way."

"You've really impressed him," Benjamin whispered in her ear as he helped her get onto her donkey. "Now, you'll be careful when you get home, won't you? You won't anger Nabal?"

"Of course not. I'm wiser now. I probably won't even speak about this to him tonight. He was drunk when I left."

"But you do plan to tell him what you've done?" Benjamin's voice was incredulous.

"If I didn't and the food could not be accounted for, some of the servants would suffer. Yes, I'll tell him. Probably in the morning."

She leaned toward her brother and felt his kiss on her cheek. She allowed herself one quick look at David and found his eyes on her face. They did not smile, but her heart was pounding when she turned her donkey's head and started up the hill toward home.

Rachel's hands were deft, unwinding the crimson scarf and unfastening the scarlet dress. "And David was willing to accept the gift?" she asked. "Did — did you see Benjamin?"

"He was willing," Abigail answered. "And yes, I saw my brother. He asked about you."

"Truly, my lady?"

"You know he loves you, don't you?"

Rachel blushed and turned away. "I hadn't thought of it, my lady."

Abigail hesitated. "I can't spare you just yet. Perhaps

when one of the other girls is better trained — or when Benjamin's life is more settled —"

"Don't worry, my lady. If such a thing is to be, it will be. Here, let me put this light robe on you for sleeping. Did you speak at all to our lord, Nabal, when you came back?"

"He was too drunk," Abigail said. "He wouldn't have known what I was talking about. I'll tell him in the morning."

"Yes, my lady. Lie down now and sleep. I know you're tired. Most of the men have also gone to sleep by now, so it ought to be quiet."

"Thank you, Rachel. Yes, I'm really very tired."

But even when she was alone in the dark, sleep was far away. Her mind was filled with a series of highly colored scenes. And the one which flashed into her consciousness again and again was the look on David's face when he watched her getting ready to leave. His eyes had been golden in the sunlight, his mouth curved with gentleness. If things were different, she might almost believe he had looked at her with love.

12

"BY ALL THE GODS, don't racket so!" Nabal's voice was rough and hoarse. "Can't you possibly put those cups on the table with less clatter?"

The young serving girl slid her eyes toward her master's flushed face and then spoke tonelessly. "I'm sorry, my lord. I'll try to be more quiet."

The tap of the clay cups on the wooden table was hardly a sound to bring on such a roar of anguish, Abigail thought. But she knew by now the intense pain that Nabal suffered on the mornings after he had drunk too much wine. Once, she had dared to point out that the dread of such pain ought to lead to temperance, but Nabal had only told her to mind her own business.

She waited, out of sight, until her husband had swallowed a little of the herb drink designed to ease his pain and had finally sat down at the table, leaning his forehead on his hands, massaging his temples with gentle fingertips. He probably wasn't fit to be approached on so serious a subject yet, but she dared not wait any longer. Within the hour, men would be coming to Nabal for instructions, advice, or judgment. If she were going to tell him of her gift to David, it was now or never. She approached the table quietly.

"My lord," she said, making her voice soft and pleasant, "I hope you slept well."

He opened his eyes briefly. "Well enough once the noise had died down. Where were you? I looked for you once during the evening. Rachel said you were busy."

"I went on an errand, my lord."

"An errand? Where?"

His voice was indifferent and for a moment, she wished desperately that she didn't have to answer, but she knew the dangers of her silence.

"I carried the food he had requested to David, the Bethlehemite, my lord."

For a few seconds, Nabal was as still as stone, his eyes still closed, his fingertips touching his temples. Then, moving slowly and stiffly, he lifted himself from his seat to stand staring at her, balancing himself with his two fists on the table.

"You *what?*"

"I was sure that my lord and his household were in danger of being killed by the desert outlaws. And I knew that my lord had simply been too — too caught up in the celebration to realize that he should never have sent the young man away with empty hands, so I —"

His face was suffused with a flood of scarlet that deepened to purple as he stared at her, his mouth open, the veins in his temples and neck knotted up and pulsing wildly.

"How dare you?" he shouted, groping for a cup to throw at her, but it seemed to elude his fingers. "I'll have you whipped — I'll —" His voice rose to a shrill shriek and he suddenly clutched his head with both hands.

Abigail stared at him in horror. The man was obviously in excruciating pain. She ran around the table toward him. "My lord, what is it?" she begged. "Here, let me help you."

Nabal's eyes were fixed and unseeing. The awful scream subsided, bubbling into silence. For what seemed like an unending second, he stood rigidly, apparently propped up by the intensity of the pain which had pierced him. Then, before she could catch him, he pitched onto the floor.

"Rachel," Abigail screamed. "Come here. I need you. Hurry!"

In a matter of seconds, she was surrounded by people — Topeleth, Rachel, Jared, and a dozen servants.

"He's dead," Topeleth said. "He's dead."

But Jared leaned forward to put his ear against his master's chest. "No, he isn't. His heart is still beating."

After crying out for Rachel, Abigail was silent. The transition from the red-faced, furious man to this rigid, unresponsive stranger whose face had slid slowly sideways into a sort of permanent leer was too abrupt, too shattering for her to take in. It was Jared who took charge, ordering Nabal's hulking attendants around as though he were their master.

"Here," he commanded. "Take his feet. And his shoulders. Be careful. Get him to his room. Hurry."

Abigail stood back and let the young man take charge. She held her cold, shaking hands clenched into fists against her mouth.

It was Rachel who finally persuaded her to move. "Come out into the sun, my lady," she coaxed. "You're cold. There's nothing to be done just now. He's had some sort of seizure. In a little while, you can go up and see what you can do."

Like a sleepwalker, Abigail allowed herself to be led into the morning sun, to be placed in a seat under an arbor of vines. The sun, splintered by the shade of moving leaves, fell warmly and comfortingly on her face and arms. In a little while, the heat would be blistering, but for this moment the sun was a source of comfort.

"My lady," Rachel begged, kneeling beside Abigail, "what happened? I heard him shouting — and then that terrible scream. What happened?"

Abigail spoke faintly. "Did anyone hear what he said? Did any of his own men hear what he said before — before he screamed?"

Rachel looked puzzled. "I don't think so, my lady. There was no one in the room except you and my lord. The serving girl was in the kitchen. What difference does it make?"

Abigail drew a long breath. "I told him about last night. He was almost mad with anger. If his men had heard, they would feel I should be whipped or even killed. It's my fault that he had the seizure."

Rachel looked over her shoulder to see that no one was near. "Now, stop, my lady. It wasn't your fault at all. His temper is always short when he's been drinking. It's only a miracle this hasn't happened long ago. Don't worry, my lady. He'll be all right when he's rested for a while."

But Abigail was remembering with dreadful clarity the way Nabal's face had slid sideways, as though a hand had smeared across wet clay, changing the shape.

"My grandfather had a seizure like that," Abigail whispered. "He never spoke or walked again. And he lived like that for three years."

Rachel stared at her mistress with horror and the dawning of pity. "Oh, my lady, maybe it will be altogether different with my lord."

Abigail leaned her head against the high back of the seat. If she were burdened with a living corpse for years, it would be no more than she deserved, she thought. How exalted she had felt, taking everything into her own hands. How sure of Yahweh's approval. And now, there was only sickness and fear in this house. No doubt Yahweh was punishing her for her arrogance, her failure to be a dutiful wife.

Rachel suddenly shook Abigail's arm. "Don't look like that, my lady. I know what you're thinking. But what if you hadn't gone? Our lord would be already dead, killed by David's sword. And this yard would be red with the blood of our lord's servants and kinsmen."

The words were as bracing as a drink of cool water. Abigail looked at her servant girl with affection and hope. "Thank you, Rachel. I had forgotten for a moment. But you're right, of course. Now, let me up so I can go and minister to my husband."

For ten long days and nights, Abigail rarely left Nabal's side. She was sure that he was conscious part of the time, and she accepted, as her due, the hatred that surfaced in his eyes. A priest was brought in to anoint Nabal with healing oil and to burn the required sacrifice. But Nabal, speechless and paralyzed, with hatred in his eyes, did not improve. On the tenth day, Abigail was sitting alone with him. She was so tired that she thought she would have to call Nabal's aunt to take her place, but something held her beside her husband. For a long time she sat quietly, occasionally sponging Nabal's face with cool water.

Suddenly she began to talk to the silent man. "I'm sorry I took matters into my own hands, my lord. But I would do it again, I know. David had vowed to kill you. I was doing it for your household, my lord."

She talked on, as though she were in a dream, blurring together apology and explanation. "I wouldn't have been such a defiant wife," she said, "if you had been sober more often. When you let me go to Hebron, I felt only gratitude toward you."

His twisted mouth twitched suddenly as though he wanted to speak. She bent over him, startled. "What is it, my lord?"

His face was still again, but it seemed to her that there was less hatred in his eyes. "I'm sorry the baby died, my lord," she whispered, her eyes blurred with sudden tears. "I'm sorry I haven't conceived another child." In weariness and unexpected grief, she lay her head down on his chest and wept quietly.

She felt a shudder run through his body, and then he was still again. But with a difference. She sat up, searching Nabal's face with terror. His eyes were open but beginning to film over with the unmistakable mark of death.

To touch him now would be to make herself unclean. But she made herself stay calm while she gently closed his eyes and pulled a linen cover up to his mouth. Then she got up to go and announce to the household that their master was dead.

"What will become of us, my lady?" Rachel's voice was

low as befitted a house still in mourning for the master who had been buried only two days before. "I've heard that our lord's brother's son will come to take over this house and our lord's business. Will you stay on with him?"

Abigail looked up and then down at her hands again. "Since my lord has no living brothers, I'm free to go back to my family, I suppose. Aunt Topeleth will probably stay on, although she *has* spoken of wishing she could be with me. I don't think she had any real affection for her other nephew or his son." She stopped a minute and then went on. "I know my parents would welcome me back. I could be a comfort to them as they grow old."

Rachel nodded. "You've always been homesick for Hebron," she murmured.

"I've sent a message to my brother," Abigail confided. "I'll wait until Jared brings word from Benjamin. Then I'll know more surely what to do."

Rachel looked up quickly and then dropped her eyes again. Abigail smiled. "Yes, this might be the time he asks for you. There *are* some wives staying with David's army, didn't you say?"

Rachel only nodded, but Abigail saw the sudden warmth in her cheeks. "If I go home," Abigail said gently, "I could spare you then. We'll see, shall we?"

They didn't have long to wait. Next day, Benjamin, accompanied by Jared and two other men, rode into the yard. Abigail, called from her room, hurried down to greet them.

"I came as soon as I could," Benjamin said.

"I knew you would." She did not offer to touch him, and he acted constrained by the presence of the other men.

"Will you come in?" Abigail asked. "Will my brother and his friends have some refreshment?"

Benjamin slid from his mule and handed the reins to Jared. The other two men followed his example, and Benjamin made a gesture toward Abigail.

"This is my sister. Abigail, these are two of David's trusted men, Aaron and Eham. They've come to speak to you."

For a minute, she stood rooted, staring. Why had David sent his men to speak to her? Why hadn't Benjamin come alone to discuss the wisdom of her returning to Hebron? Were they planning to take more food now that Nabal could no longer refuse?

Remembering her manners, she led the way into the house. "If you will sit here, my lords," she said, "I'll have some wine brought. Please be comfortable in my — in the house of Nabal."

When she came back with a jug of wine and several cups, the men were talking. She didn't catch any words, but she heard a muted rumble of laughter.

"May I serve my lords?" she asked.

The man Aaron looked up at her. "It would be better, I think, if you sat down, my lady. There, is that your girl in the doorway?"

Abigail glanced up, saw Rachel, and nodded.

"Then let her come to serve the wine," Aaron said. "I bring a message from David of Bethlehem. It may seem very soon after the death of your husband, but David has trained himself to move with the swiftness of a military man."

Abigail looked at the man with astonishment. She had no idea what he was talking about.

Aaron, dark and burly, looked steadily into Abigail's face as he said, "Since you are a widow now, David has sent us to ask you to be his wife."

She felt a sudden pounding in her head, and the faces of the three men tilted and blurred in front of her eyes.

Benjamin half rose as though to move toward her, but she shook her head. As suddenly as the faintness had come over her, it left, and she was calm and steady.

Rising to her feet, she said clearly, "May your maidservant be as a maid to wash the feet of David's servants." With steady hands, she lifted a basin of water from the floor and moved toward the men. Rachel made a move to take the basin, but Abigail shook her head. By performing this humble task, she could demonstrate her total willingness to submit to David's wish.

Somehow she kept her mind empty until she had finished washing and drying the feet of David's men. Then looking up at Aaron, she said, "Tell my lord David I will come."

Aaron's expression was rueful. "I was wrong," he said to Benjamin. "I thought she'd wring her hands and wail about leaving her good house and her soft life."

Benjamin grinned. "I tried to tell you, but you wouldn't listen."

Abigail stood up in silence, her heart hammering with thick, swift strokes. She couldn't believe this was really happening, but at the same time, she felt as though all of her life had been moving toward this hour.

"May I speak to her alone?" Benjamin asked.

The other two nodded, and Benjamin took Abigail's arm and led her out of the room. He had hardly looked at Rachel, and yet Abigail knew he was not unaware of her.

"I'll bring Rachel with me," Abigail promised. "Will that please you?"

Benjamin seemed to be having difficulty saying what he wanted to say. "We'll talk of that later. Now, there's something you have to know."

"What?"

"You won't be David's only wife." He spoke abruptly, almost roughly.

"I know that. I know he married Michal, daughter of Saul. But she's been given to someone else, I heard."

"Not Michal. Another one. Ahinoam from Jezreel. He married her only a matter of weeks before you brought the food to us. She's nothing like you. She's a tall, shy girl — little more than a child. Pretty enough but timid. Rumor has it that she's already with child. Can you — can you live with that?"

Abigail spoke slowly, groping for the words. "Yahweh wouldn't have led me to David if He hadn't wanted it to happen. He wouldn't have taken Nabal's life if He hadn't wanted me to be free. Whether being a second wife is what I want or not doesn't matter. What matters is that I'm an instrument in the hands of the Lord."

"That's exactly what David predicted you'd say. I wasn't so sure. In spite of the way Nabal treated you, you were mistress of this house. So — I just wasn't sure."

Abigail stood looking at her brother with her chin high. She was confident that he hadn't guessed the pain that had daggered through her when he told her about Ahinoam. The pain was something she would keep hidden, even from Rachel.

"Tell David," Abigail said shortly, "that I will come as soon as I can get ready. Tell him I'll hurry."

She turned to run quickly toward her room, but whether she was hurrying to leave Nabal's house or hurrying to the abode of David, she didn't know. She didn't even want to know.

13

THERE WAS NO CEREMONIAL GREETING waiting for
Abigail at David's camp. The men who met her small caravan
(Topeleth had decided at the last minute to come with her,
and they had brought three serving girls in addition to
Rachel) were courteous, but there was no sign of celebration.

"Our lord David has been called out to battle," one of the
men explained, helping Abigail get down from her donkey.
"It's only a skirmish, but a troop of Amalekites from the
south came up into Judean land. David has gone to deal
with them."

She longed to ask when he would return, but she held
back the words. Looking around, she saw that the camp
was situated on a small plateau, protected on one side by
cliffs notched with caves and on another side by a precipitous
drop to the valley below. The only easy entrance to the
place was through the narrow pass on the side toward
Maon, and even there, the terrain was rough enough to
make her grateful for the sure-footed donkeys.

But it was the fourth side of the camp that caught her
attention. From some hidden source above them, a cascade
of clear water came springing over the rocks, tumbling
toward the valley. Along its banks, trees and bushes grew
in what was almost a lush profusion, and the air was cool
and sweet. She had heard many times of En Gedi, the living

water that fell into the Dead Sea. This was the first time she
had ever seen it.

Glancing at the other women to see if they were as
enchanted with the miracle of En Gedi as she was, she saw
that Topeleth was looking at the wild setting with an
expression of fear. *Maybe she'll have to be taken back to
Nabal's house,* Abigail thought, *if she finds wilderness
living too hard.* But Abigail herself was experiencing a
feeling of homecoming, combined with a sense of destiny
fulfilled. Hadn't she known, since she was a girl and Samuel
had visited her father's house in Hebron, that Yahweh had
intended her to do something special for David? She must
have been brought here for that purpose.

"Is my brother with my lord?" she asked, turning back to
the soldier.

"Yes, my lady. Benjamin always goes along. They ought
to be back well before dark if everything goes all right."

She swallowed her disappointment over David's absence.
"I would like to refresh myself after the journey," she said.
"Is there any place where my women and I may have
privacy?"

"Yes, my lady. Over there. Do you see the wide opening
in the cliff? There's a big cave there — dry and airy — even
with partitions that separate it into rooms. It's where the
cooking is done and the weaving and grinding. The women
stay there mostly. Except at night. Then they go with their
husbands."

"And if they have no husbands?" Her hand moved toward
Topeleth and the serving girls.

The soldier grinned. "Then there's room in there for them
to sleep. But good-looking wenches such as these may have
husbands before you know it."

Abigail spoke stiffly. "I will not have my girls molested."

The soldier looked affronted. "You don't have to worry,
my lady. The men are under strict military discipline."

Abigail only nodded and shepherded the women toward
the cave that had been pointed out, but in spite of her

appearance of calm, her heart was beating erratically. Ahinoam of Jezreel would probably be among the women in that cave, and how was it going to be to meet the girl who carried David's child? Abigail felt as much apprehension as she had felt the day she had become Nabal's wife.

But when the moment of meeting came, her fears were unjustified. Ahinoam was scarlet with shyness, her greeting so humble that Abigail was embarrassed.

"My lady," Ahinoam said. She bowed awkwardly.

"Don't refer to me so," Abigail said. "You're the first wife here."

Ahinoam smiled, and Abigail felt a stab of compassion for the scarlet-cheeked girl who stood facing her.

"I'm with child," Ahinoam confided naively, "so my lord has done his duty, you see. He doesn't — I haven't seen him for —" She blundered to a stop.

"Don't worry," Abigail said gently.

"And you'll be my friend?" Ahinoam asked. "Will you be my friend, my lady?"

"If you'll call me Abigail," Abigail said, feeling years older than the dark-skinned girl in front of her, although there was probably no more than two or three years difference in their ages.

Ahinoam sighed with relief. "I've been so worried," she confided. "Ever since the day he came back with the gifts from your hand, I've been so worried."

The other women crowded around them then, and Abigail said all the right words of greeting, but Ahinoam's last words rang through her head again and again. "Ever since the day he came back with the gifts," she had said. But Nabal had still been alive, and she hadn't been a widow then. What did it mean? Did she dare to hope that David had been drawn to her as, long before she saw him, she had been drawn to him?

While the women chattered, Abigail felt her tension building. *If only Benjamin were here,* she thought. Benjamin could tell her why, with Ahinoam for his comfort, David had sought a second wife. The girl might be almost tongue-tied with shyness, but she was really very pretty. Oh, of course, kings had more than one wife, but David wasn't a king yet.

But he will be some day, she thought. *And if he is to be king, then he needs the loyalty of all the tribes of Israel.* So he had taken a Jezreelite from the north and a Calebite from the south. It was only politics that had made him do what he had done — and she had come running at the crook of his finger.

As I would do again, she thought. She got up and followed Rachel to the cave that had been pointed out as David's.

"You're to take your things there," Ahinoam had announced in a voice that seemed to hold no jealousy at all.

"Thank you," Abigail had said, knowing already that she could not be so calm if David's politics or desires led him to another woman without a backward look at her.

It was nearly dark before the sounds of returning soldiers clattered through the camp. Abigail, dressed in white trimmed with scarlet, looked across the cave to where Rachel busied herself putting her mistress's belongings up on dry ledges.

Rachel returned the look, the apprehension on her face matching Abigail's. "He's coming, my lady," she whispered.

"Well, certainly not right away. They'll eat, I should think."

"And he'll surely bathe himself in the stream before he comes here," Rachel said, her words running together rapidly. "The fresh stream here at En Gedi is like a miracle, isn't it, my lady?" Rachel did not meet her mistress's eyes. "Such a vast, dry wilderness — and then, suddenly, this rush of fresh water and green trees beside it."

Abigail smiled. She had finally recognized Rachel's chattering for what it was. The girl was as nervous and tense as Abigail herself. Benjamin had ridden off to do battle, also.

"If my brother speaks for you tonight, are you willing to go to him?"

"I'll do whatever you bid me do," Rachel said cautiously, but her eyes were bright.

"Let's sit down," Abigail suggested, "and wait for what will happen. Here, sit beside me."

Shyly, Rachel sat on the ledge of the rock which apparently served as seats, as strips of woven wool rugs had been spread over them. The girls were silent, watching the cave opening.

Is Rachel as frightened as I am? Abigail thought. *Is her heart knocking against her chest as though it wanted to get out, the way mine is?* But she knew that if Rachel's heart was pounding, it wasn't out of fear. Rachel *knew* she was loved.

It was Benjamin who came to them first. Still dirty and disheveled from his strenuous day, he came no closer than the door of the cave. "So you really came?" he asked.

"Of course. You knew I would."

"And have you met Ahinoam?" Benjamin's questions obviously stemmed from the worry that had not left him.

"She's a sweet girl," Abigail said. "I don't think you need to worry. I've always known that — that kings had more than one wife."

Benjamin's face showed relief. "As long as you understand, then. And — what of Rachel? Will you let her wed me?"

They spoke as though the girl were not even in the cave.

"It seems there will be very little chance here for a marriage ceremony," Abigail said. "Do you mean to just take her tonight?"

Benjamin looked offended. "Tomorrow or the next day, when there's no fighting, when there's time to prepare some sort of a feast and I can announce my intentions as David has already done about you, and when I've found a cave that promises privacy, then I'll take her as my wife."

"Without Father's permission?"

"Father has known for a long time that I wanted her."

In the dim, flickering light of the fire at the mouth of the cave, Abigail saw Rachel's sudden radiance.

"Besides," Benjamin went on, "David will act as sponsor. He approves of marriage for his men. He knows a man is steadier if he has a woman to come home to."

"Then you have my blessing, too," Abigail said. "Perhaps

you'll escort her over to the women's quarters now? I'll wait
here for my lord David."

Rachel spoke for the first time. "But, my lady, ought you
to be alone? Won't you be afraid?"

"Have I ever been afraid of caves?" Abigail asked. "With
a good fire at the mouth — and a camp swarming with
brave men? I'll enjoy it. See, my lyre is here. I'll sing a while
— and think of home."

Rachel went then with a glow about her that lit a
responsive glow in Benjamin's eyes. Abigail saw that they
walked discreetly apart, but their joy was clearly evident.

Even for Rachel, Abigail thought with a wistfulness she
had not anticipated, *there will be some manner of feast. But for
me there is nothing. Nothing to make me feel like a bride.*

The lyre, held against her body, made a soft, sweet
strumming in the night, and Abigail bent her head over it in
an attitude of listening.

"The skies are lit by Yahweh's hand," she chanted,
searching for chords that would fit the words. "Yahweh
placed the stars across the night."

"They told me you could sing. They hadn't told me how
sweetly."

It was David's voice. Somehow, she kept herself from
making a startled movement, and her hands became very
still on the strings.

"My lord," she said.

"Is it your own song?" He was still standing in the cave
opening, the fire lighting his face from below so that she
could see the strong line of his jaw and the brilliance of his
eyes.

"Yes, my lord. Only it's not really a song yet. I was just,"
her voice faltered. "I was just waiting until you came, my
lord."

David moved around the fire and came closer to her. She
saw that his hands were full. He was carrying bread and
figs and a small wine bottle, as though he were a servant,
not a would-be king.

"Well, now I'm here," he said. He sat down beside her on the ledge, placing the food on the floor, and she saw that he carried something else, a spray of flowers.

"I bathed in the stream," he explained, "and a tamarisk tree was in bloom. I pulled a few blossoms for your hair. You've been cheated out of all the excitement of a wedding celebration."

"It's all right, my lord." She looked up at him, but his eyes were so intent on her face that she looked down again at the floor.

She felt his fingers fastening the stems of the flowers into her hair, and she was astonished at the gentleness of his hands. Could this be a man who had spent the day in battle, presumably killing his enemy?

"You're lovelier than I remembered," he said softly, and his hands slid down her cheeks to cup her chin and pull it up so that her eyes were forced to meet his. "Did that lout of a husband of yours ever tell you how beautiful you are?"

She tried to smile, but she felt her lips quivering. "My husband didn't talk to me much."

David bent his head and brushed her lips lightly with his. "I can believe it," he said. He sat away from her and clasped his arms around his knees. "Do you understand why I asked you to be my wife?"

"I think so, my lord," she said steadily. "Ahinoam brings the goodwill of the Jezreelites, and I bring you the loyalty of Hebron as well as the goodwill of the Calebites at Maon."

"I don't deny it," he said. "But it's more than that. Ever since I first saw you, I wanted *you*. The fact that you bring double loyalty is only my good fortune."

"Or Yahweh's gift, my lord?"

"Or Yahweh's gift," he agreed. "The girl, Ahinoam, is pleasant enough and even comely, but so shy that she can't — or won't talk to me. Fortunately, she's already with child, so I don't have to think about her again. I'm free to think about you."

She faced him bravely. "I may not be what you think, my

lord. I did not have a happy marriage — so — so I may only be as dull and good as you say Ahinoam is."

David threw back his head and laughed. "You've already shown more wit and understanding in these few minutes than she did in all the weeks she shared my bed." He stretched his arms above his head. "By thunder, I'm tired! It was a brutal fight."

He dropped his hands onto his lap, palms up, in an oddly defenseless gesture. "I *hate* the killing," he confided, "but at the same time, I know the killing has to be done. It leaves me — empty."

"Would you like me to sing to you, my lord?" She felt a wave of shyness, remembering Samuel's words about David's singing. "I know Samuel said you were the sweetest singer in Israel — but if you'd like, I could sing for you."

David smiled. "It's tempting," he admitted, "but there will be many times for you to sing to me. For now, let's eat something. I've had nothing since early morning, and I'm famished. While I eat, tell me a little about your home in Hebron — about your parents. Tell me a little about yourself."

She took the offered fig from his hand and nibbled it slowly while she tried to do as he had asked. No man had ever asked her to talk about herself, and she was too shy to do more than touch the surface of her life.

"My father spoiled me," she finished with a smile. "He let me help him watch the sheep. I spent more time in the wilderness than in the house."

"Then this cave doesn't distress you?"

"Nothing here distresses me, my lord."

He had been drinking wine from the skin as she said this, but he took it away from his mouth. "Nothing?"

She shook her head, and he held out the wineskin for her to drink. She had to cup her hands around his to steady the skin so that no wine would be spilled on her robe.

David was quiet for a minute. Then he carefully stoppered the skin with its thong and put the remnants of food into a niche on a high shelf.

"My bed is back here," he said abruptly, reaching down his hand to pull her to her feet. "Is the lyre safe or must it be wrapped against the night?"

She felt his excitement in the way his fingers tightened on hers. Nabal probably wouldn't have cared enough to ask about the lyre and certainly wouldn't have waited for an answer, but she dared to say, "It should be wrapped, my lord."

David laughed. "A good lyre can't be spoiled. Love will wait a few minutes, no?"

Her fingers fumbled with the wrappings for the lyre, and then she felt David's fingers holding the lyre steady, turning it to accept the wrapping.

"Thank you, my lord," she said.

"Thank *you*, my love," he said.

No one had ever called her that before. And what else had he said? That he had *wanted* her.

With a singing heart, she put her hand into David's and followed him into the back of the cave, feeling more like a bride than she had ever felt sitting under the little tent, with almond blossoms in her hair, waiting for Nabal to take her away.

part III

Then David said to himself, "Now I will perish one day by the hand of Saul. There is nothing better for me than to escape into the land of the Philistines. . . . And David lived with Achish at Gath, he and his men, each with his household, even David with his two wives, Ahinoam . . . and Abigail.

1 Samuel 27:1a, 3

14

THE RUMORS HAD RACED through the camp all day. No soldiers had returned with definite reports, and yet everyone seemed to know that this was the day when David and Saul would finally come face to face.

For every woman who wept in fear that her man or David himself might die by Saul's hand, another woman made boast that it would be Saul who would fall, pierced by David's spear.

"The whole thing is ridiculous," Abigail snapped to Rachel as they sat inside the mouth of David's cave, mending sandals. Her nerves were frayed to breaking, so that her voice was harsh and accusing. "David would never touch Saul — everyone who has ever listened to him knows that. And Yahweh intends David to be king of Israel, so will He let him be cut down in the wilderness?"

Rachel, whose face was pale and tense, spoke soothingly. "Don't worry about the rumors. Our lord David talks to you more than anyone — even Joab, I think, and Joab is the chief captain of the army. So you're the one who knows. Don't fret, my — my sister."

Abigail tried to smile. "When you've reached the place where you can say 'Abigail' freely, then I'll know some sort of miracle has happened."

Rachel grinned and a hint of color came into her cheeks.

"I'm sorry, Abigail. I called you 'my lady' for so long that it still seems wrong to call you by your name."

"Even when you've been my sister for three months?"

Rachel only nodded and looked again in the direction the men had gone. "Do you think Saul is really out there?" she asked.

"David said so," Abigail answered. "His spies had reported that Saul had at least three thousand soldiers scouring the whole area, looking for us."

"Wouldn't you think they'd come directly here — to En Gedi? It seems so logical to me that David would choose this place where the water is."

"It wouldn't seem logical to Saul. His mind is so devious and twisted that he doesn't think clearly."

"But his captain — Abner, isn't it? Wouldn't he guess?"

Abigail shook her head. "It's too obvious. My lord, David, says that no one would believe we have enough courage to stay in this green and lovely place. They're searching in the most desolate areas of the wilderness. They must think the armies of David live like animals."

"But David has gone out to meet them," Rachel said. "If he doesn't intend to harm Saul — if he has no heart to kill the king — then why did he go out to fight him? Why didn't they stay safely here?"

Abigail spoke slowly. "I suppose they knew Saul's army would eventually come here. I think my lord has gone to lead them away from the camp — away from the women."

Ahinoam spoke hesitantly from the cave opening. "May I come in, Abigail? May I sit and talk a while?"

Abigail sighed inwardly. Rachel's eyes twinkled at her as Abigail called out, "Of course, my sister. Come in. We're just sitting here out of the sun, mending some sandal straps. We ought to be working over in the kitchens, but we were hot and weary and —"

"And worried," Ahinoam finished for her. "I know. Me, too. If our lord is killed, who will take care of us?"

Abigail felt the words run through her like a blade. "Our lord will *not* be killed," she snapped. "Don't *say* that!"

"I'm sorry," Ahinoam muttered. She sat gingerly. "The child moves every day now," she announced. "Did your child move so when you carried him, Abigail?"

The temptation was strong to say, "Of course. All babies move so!" But Ahinoam was only hurt if anyone were short with her, and nothing improved the quality of her conversation.

Before Abigail could frame a suitable answer, there came a sharp, clear call. It was the sentry's signal that something had been sighted.

"Wait. Listen," Abigail said. She sat still, her head bent, waiting for the next sound. If there was danger, the sentry would shout twice and everyone would flee into the largest cave. If the sighted army was David's men returning, the shout would be louder and there would be three cries of triumph.

For a few seconds, the silence swelled up around them, so that Abigail felt she could hear the pounding of her heart. Then the sentry's cry came three times — loud, shrill, triumphant.

"They're coming back," Rachel breathed, and Abigail could see that the girl's hands were clasped in thankfulness.

"Then we're safe," Ahinoam said in the self-centered voice of a child.

But Abigail waited in silence until the men — a few riding ahead, the others walking — came crowding through the narrow pass that guarded their campsite. For a second she was almost afraid to look, but then she lifted her head. He was there, at the head of his men, as he always was, his red gold hair glinting in the sun, a grin on his face, his spear held aloft like a banner.

"Come," she said, holding her voice level with effort. "Come. We've been lazy long enough. We've got to hurry and prepare food for our men. From the looks of things, they've come home victorious."

The evening meal was a celebration. The men were laughing, even getting rowdy at times. There seemed to be some huge joke among them, referred to only by innuendo, but it evidently delighted them and made them regard David with more admiration than usual. That every one of these men would die for David a dozen times over had been obvious to Abigail from the day she had arrived at the camp. But tonight they were plainly excited over something their leader had done, to the point that they were in higher spirits than she had ever known them to be.

The women, thoroughly contented over the fact that all of the men had come home, hurried back and forth from the kitchen area to where the men ate, sprawled on the ground. None of them, not even Abigail, tried to make sense out of the raucous talk and laughter. Most of them were contented just to know the men were safe, and Abigail knew she would hear about it when she and David were alone. He had met her eyes once with a glance as intimate as the touch of a hand, and then he had turned to his men and paid no further attention to her.

She was used to this by now. A war leader who concerned himself with his wives in front of his men was only asking for disrespect. And David was a leader of men before he was anything else. But in the privacy of their cave — shared every night until now she no longer even felt a sense of guilt over his neglect of Ahinoam — they talked. She had discovered that there were men, besides her father and brother, who could be gentle and warm and whose mind spoke to hers.

"There couldn't have been a battle," Rachel murmured once to Abigail as they passed each other. "Not a single man has even been hurt. Yet they act as though they had won some great victory."

"Be patient. Benjamin will tell you all about it."

"Knowing Benjamin, he'll be disappointed if he didn't have a chance to break a few heads," Rachel responded with a wry smile.

Abigail glanced over at her brother. Rachel was probably right, but certainly Benjamin didn't look discontented. Whatever had happened that day, the men were happy about it.

Even David. He didn't look like this after an ordinary battle. Always before he had been — what had he said the first night they were together? —empty. Tonight, however, he looked anything but empty. Anyhow, she could do nothing now but try to be patient until the men had finished their merrymaking and had gone to bed. Then she would find out.

She was almost grateful for the work that had to be done and would keep her busy until bedtime. As the leader's wife, she had been granted respect and even affection, but she always worked along with the other women. All the girls who had come with her from Nabal's house were married to soldiers now and so had achieved a position higher than that of serving girl. This had created an odd sort of democracy among the women — flawed occasionally by jealousies and petty quarrels — but strong enough to hold them together without the familiar structure of parent and child, mistress and slave.

"Here," someone said, and Abigail turned to take a jar that was being thrust at her. "This needs filling."

It was Topeleth, working as hard as anyone. To Abigail's astonishment, she had made the adjustment to wilderness life and was a sturdy source of common sense when the younger women needed advice.

This, at least, Nabal gave me, Abigail thought, smiling at the older woman. But she knew that Nabal had given her more than a loving aunt. He had given her, through his harshness, a strength she could never have learned from her parents' love.

"Abigail?" David's voice was pitched low as he came in the mouth of the cave.

"Back here, my lord."

Sure-footed in the near dark — there were only a few coals left in the fire — he made his way to where woolen rugs and goatskins were spread on the ground to make a bed. She stood up to meet him, and his arms came around her as though they had been separated for months. She returned his kiss with all the depth of her love, a depth which she had never dared put into words.

"You smell good," he murmured. "You must have washed your hair."

"With all the men gone, we women dared to take a long bath in the stream today," she said, smiling. "It's not always possible, you know."

He laughed and kissed her again and then pulled her down to sit on the rugs. "Well, at least you would all have been clean for our funerals if we had died in combat."

Her voice was fierce. "Don't *say* that! Don't even think it." She held on to him so tightly that he said gently and with some surprise, "Why, Abigail. I was only teasing."

"I can't joke about your dying," she said.

He stroked her hair back from her face and kissed her reassuringly. When he spoke, his voice was matter-of-fact. "Well, but we didn't die. There wasn't even a battle."

"You mean, Saul really wasn't out there? But your spies —"

"Oh, Saul was out there, all right," he said. "Saul and at least three thousand of his men. And I met him. I was almost as close to him as I am to you."

"And he didn't try to kill you?"

She felt, rather than heard, David's laughter. "He didn't even know I was there."

She pulled herself out of his arms and tried to speak sternly. "Please, my lord, tell me what happened."

David sighed and lay back on the skins, pulling her down beside him. She put her head in the hollow of his shoulder and prepared to listen.

"We came up with Saul yesterday where he was camped on the hill of Hachilah," David said. He had a gift for words, and Abigail listened, as she always did, with deep appreciation for the vivid way her husband talked. "You know how my men travel — I've told you before — as lightly and silently as ghosts. No one in Saul's camp had any idea that we were within miles of them. Joab advised against attacking, even though we had the element of surprise. It's foolish to pit six hundred men against three thousand."

"Joab isn't always cautious," Abigail said.

"Nor would I want him to be. Caution never won a battle. Well, anyhow, I gave the command to fall back a short distance for the night. But later, I took Abishai with me. He volunteered," he added, "and we went back toward Saul's camp."

"Not Joab, but his brother, Abishai?"

"Joab had to stay with the troops. He didn't want me to leave, but I gave him no choice in the matter. Abishai and I moved like shadows until we lay on the hill opposite from Saul."

"It was dark then?" she asked.

"Yes, dark. Except that the stars hung low and showed the shape of the land. And, of course, there were fires in Saul's camp. Fires bright enough to show me where the king lay sleeping, surrounded by a circle of his followers. I could even see Abner's gray beard. He was lying closest to the king."

Abigail felt a chill creep over her skin. "Well, but that wasn't as close as you are to me, my lord," she argued. "There was a valley between you, wasn't there?"

"And I wasn't holding him in my arms," David agreed with a soft laugh. "Anyhow, I motioned to Abishai that I was going to make my way over to Saul's camp. He was obligated to follow me, although I'm sure he thought it was madness."

She sat up, propping herself on her elbow. "You went into Saul's camp? Truly, my lord?"

He pulled her back down to her former position. "Yes, truly. You can see I'm safe and unharmed."

She touched his cheek for reassurance. "Go on," she whispered.

"It was rough going," David admitted. "The starlight showed the general shape of the land, but the valley was stony and treacherous. Several times I thought one or the other of us would break a leg. But Yahweh was with us, and we made it safely to the top of the hill. In no time at all, I was standing beside Saul, looking down at him, remembering all the days he had smiled on me as a father does."

David's voice was pensive. Abigail wondered if David had also been thinking of the fiery Michal who had been his wife, and of Jonathan, who had been David's dearest friend. But all she said was, "And they didn't wake, my lord?"

"I think Yahweh must have caused a deep sleep to fall on all of them. The more I think about it, the more I realize that what happened wasn't natural at all."

"What did you do?" she asked.

"Abishai begged to kill King Saul. He couldn't believe that I would just stand there with the king delivered into my hand and not do anything about it. He said he could kill Saul with one blow — that the king would never know he had been struck — but I stopped him." He spoke with sudden anxiety. "*You* understand, don't you? You understand that I can't lift my hand against the Lord's anointed?"

"Who better than I?" Abigail said. "Remember how I begged you not to take vengeance into your hands against Nabal? How could I approve your taking vengeance against Saul, in spite of what he's done to us?"

She felt him relax. "I tried to explain that when we got back to our camp, but Joab thought I was foolish. Oh, the men were all amused and proud of the way it turned out, but Joab thinks I was sentimental."

"Let him think it. You know what you are."

"How did I manage before you came?" David marveled. He kissed her softly.

"But if you didn't kill the king, what did you do?" Abigail asked.

"We took his spear — it was stuck in the ground right beside his head — and his water jug, and we climbed back across the valley and took up our place on the opposite hill. The sun came up like molten gold, and we could clearly see the camp waking up and shaking itself like a dog that has slept too long. When Abner's gray head lifted, I stood and shouted at him."

"You didn't!"

"Ah, but I did," David said cheerfully. "I accused him of failing to take care of the king. I showed them the spear and the water jug, and make no mistake about it, they recognized them and were properly awed."

"But the king? What did he do?"

David's mirth ebbed away. "He recognized my voice. He called me 'son' and admitted he had been a fool to chase me down as though I were truly his enemy."

Her voice was incredulous. "In front of all of his men, he admitted he had been a fool?"

"He did. What's more, he swore he would no longer seek me out, and he predicted I would be successful and prevail."

"Oh, my lord! Now we can stop being afraid."

"I wish it were so. But Saul no longer has the Spirit of Yahweh in him, and the spirit of darkness which rules him will make him my enemy again whenever it pleases. We'll never be truly safe from Saul, my love, until he's dead. And I'm not the one to bring on his death."

"Then — we'll stay here in the wilderness," she said. "We'll plant some grain in that watered valley and live here until Saul is no longer king."

"And you won't long for a fine house such as Nabal gave? You won't wish for costly possessions?" His voice was teasing.

"I long for nothing, as long as my lord and I are together."

David ran his hand along the length of her arm, captured her hand, and held it against his lips. "I still can't believe my luck in getting a woman like you — one who has a mind as good as a man's — a woman who understands me."

"Then perhaps — " her voice was very low — "perhaps you'll still need me for *that* — when you — take other wives."

"I may take other wives," David said, "but I think it will only be for politics, and I'll visit them out of a sense of duty so that children may be born. But I will always want and need you. Can you doubt it?"

"I don't know what the future holds," she said.

"But you seemed to know that day you brought the food — the day you prophesied that I would be ruler of all Israel."

She was quiet for a minute. She knew that the words she had said to David that day were words given to her by Yahweh. Oh, they may have been shaped by Samuel's predictions and by her own dreams, but the conviction that David would be king, that his life would be spared while his enemies fell about him, had come directly from Yahweh.

"I *did* know," she said at last. "Yahweh gave me the words, and I know they were true. But He never told me — never told me whether or not David would love me."

"Well, David does love you," the man said, drawing her closer to him. "And whether I take other wives for politics or love, you will always matter to me."

She drew a deep breath. David's voice was sincere, and his intentions were noble, she knew. For what they were worth, she would take these words for her comfort and remember them always.

"Yes, my lord. And you — you will always matter to me."

"And for that I'm happy," David said. "Now, enough talking for one night. In a day or two, when I've had time to make some plans, I have something important to discuss with you. I need *your* reaction before I even place the idea before Joab. But for now, though, come and kiss me, my love."

And she went, not sure whether she found more joy in the touch of his hands or the knowledge that he trusted her opinion and wanted her help in the shaping of his plans.

15

"SAUL WILL KILL YOU someday! The more he learns about this part of the country, the more certain he is of meeting up with us."

The speaker, Joab, leaned toward David. They had been arguing for a long time and were both very weary.

"Why do we go over this again and again?" David asked. "Do you think I haven't told myself that Saul might kill me someday? Do you think I haven't faced it?"

"Then why did you let him escape when you had his life in your hand, my lord?" Joab asked, exasperation making his voice rough.

David's voice was cold. "Must my nephew be reminded that I am the leader here?"

"It's only my concern for my lord that makes it necessary for me to speak so boldly. But if you, yourself, have faced up to the danger of Saul, surely you agree that something will have to be done. Your spies have reported that he's already talking of bringing an army into the wilderness again. Before the next moon waxes and wanes, Saul and his thousands may be trampling us into the dirt."

David was silent, and Joab went on with even greater intensity. "I know you hope that your friendship with Jonathan will prevent a major battle. Frankly, I don't believe that Jonathan has any real influence on his father."

David sighed deeply. "Jonathan hasn't had any real influence on his father since I left. He is, in a sense, as much of an outlaw as I am. He hasn't any more access to his father's thoughts than I have to his father's house."

"Then he couldn't keep Saul from tracking you down, my lord."

David did not answer for a long time. He was turned away from Joab as though he did not want his nephew to see the marks of pain that were suddenly etched on his face.

"So what do you suggest?" David asked at last.

"I don't know, my lord. A surprise attack isn't feasible if you continue to insist that no one dare touch the king. I can't see any other possibility except finding another place to hide — far from this place, far from anywhere Saul might look."

David nodded. "I've been thinking of it myself. I'm not quite as stupid as you think."

"My lord," Joab cried, "I never said that. I would never think it."

"You think many things," David said flatly. "But I know your concern for me is real. When I've thought my plan through, I'll talk to you about it."

"When you've discussed it with Nabal's widow, you mean," Joab retorted. "I wonder, my lord, at the wisdom of talking over such matters with a woman."

David stared at Joab. "Abigail is my wife, not Nabal's widow. I hope I don't need to remind you of that again. She is both discreet and wise, and was sent to me, I believe, by Yahweh."

"Yes, my lord," Joab mumbled. "I don't mean to anger David. I've been faithful since the days in Bethlehem when we played together in the fields, watching the sheep."

"Yes, yes, I know. You don't have to remind me. I'll always be grateful to you — but I have to do things my way, not yours. Even if I offend you."

"My lord cannot offend his servant," Joab said. "I'll try to be patient until you can tell me your plans." He got up.

"Good," David said. "I'll call you when I want you." He narrowed his eyes, watching his commander turn to leave. "Remember, my nephew," he called after Joab, making his voice gentle, "I depend on you. I always will."

Joab's face brightened, and his shoulders straightened. He sketched his uncle a small salute of farewell and moved across the camp.

The first rains of winter had started to fall, and Abigail stood in the mouth of David's cave, watching the blowing sheets of rain. She had planned to sit out under the evening sky and make some music. Since David was closeted with Joab in the men's council cave, there was really nothing to keep her in her own place. She supposed she could throw a scarf over her head and dash to the large cave where some of the women gathered to talk or work with the cloth, but she didn't want to listen to their petty concerns. She really longed for the silence of dusk and the sweet sound of her lyre. A new song had been hammering in her head all day, a song whose meaning was still unknown.

Well, there was nothing to it but to stay in the cave and make her music there, even though the lyre sounded dull shut inside the stone walls.

She sat on a low ledge and pulled her lyre against her body. She had tried to play David's once, and they had both been reduced to helpless laughter by the awkward way she strummed it. Hers was lighter and smaller, more suited to her hands.

The first strummed chords were as sweet as love, and for a few minutes she drifted in a dream of growing old beside David, with children to bless their hearth and no responsibility greater than the health of an ailing ewe.

Then her sturdy realism shredded the dream and forced her to face the future more honestly. David would be king, and it was her duty to serve him in some special way. She still wasn't sure what she was supposed to do. She could only hope that someday Yahweh would make it clear. Yahweh — God of her parents, God of her heart.

"Yahweh, ruler of Israel," she sang. "Yahweh, mighty God of earth and sky. Hear us, Lord of mercy. Hear us —" A note came discordantly, and she stopped to play it again, humming the melody.

The next words came out without any deliberate intent on her part. It was as though they had been poured into her mind from an unseen vessel. "Stay with us, Lord of Israel," she sang. "As we live in unclean places, as we eat at the tables of the uncircumcised, shelter us. Hold us, Yahweh, Lord, in the hollow of Your hand."

David's voice came so abruptly that she jumped. "What are you singing? How did you know?"

She turned, bewildered, to face him. "It's only a song that's been building in my mind all day, my lord. How did I know what?"

David was obviously shaken. "That we would live in unclean places, that we would eat at the table of the uncircumcised?"

"I don't know what you're talking about, my lord. It was only a song that came from nowhere."

David shook his head. "It came from Yahweh. You had no way of knowing. No one knows what I've been thinking."

She put her lyre down and went over to David. With gentle hands, she pulled him down to sit on the ledge and then sat beside him. "You're tired, my lord. I'm sorry if my song has upset you. Sit quietly and I'll sing something else. Perhaps, in a short while, you can play your lyre and we'll sing together. Would you like that?"

"You know what you remind me of?" David said. "You remind me of myself when I first came to Saul — young and sure that the beauty of my singing could cure his every ill."

"I've never claimed my singing was beautiful, my lord," she said stiffly.

"Oh, I know, I know. It's just — listen, Abigail, that song of yours. Can you sing it again?"

"If it won't offend my lord." Her voice was still rigid with hurt.

David clenched his fists and shouted, "Women! The best and loveliest are still maddening! Jonathan and I talked about it once — about how a man can't really be friends with a woman. Not unless he's always willing to play the lover, too. It's why friendship with a man can be so comfortable."

"I should wish then that I were a man," Abigail muttered.

"Yahweh forbid!" David's voice lightened, and his hands drew her close. "I want you just the way you are. Even with your silly need to be assured that your singing could never offend me."

His lips brushed hers, and for a few seconds he held her close to him. Then she drew away and began to strum the strings of the lyre.

When she came to the lines "when we live in unclean places, when we eat at the table of the uncircumcised," David stopped her.

"And you truly don't know where you got the words?" he said.

"No, my lord, truly."

"You didn't know that I have decided that we'll pack up everything we have and go and throw in our lot with Achish of Gath, king of the Philistines?"

His voice was harsh, and his fingers gripped her arm so hard that she winced from the pain. David didn't even notice. He was staring intently at her.

"Do you understand what I'm saying?" he demanded.

"Yes, my lord," she whispered. "But — my lord — the Philistines are our enemy."

"Not necessarily," David said. "It depends on who you mean when you say 'our.'"

"I mean we who are from Israel and Judah. I mean we who are the people of Yahweh. I mean we who are of the Covenant."

David stood up and took a restless turn about the cave. "You don't have to go on and on," he said impatiently.

"Your first answer was more than adequate. I, myself, was thinking only of our group here in En Gedi. Perhaps Achish could be persuaded that *we* are not his enemy."

"Does Yahweh want you to go?" she asked. "Do you feel in your heart that Yahweh approves?"

Her questions were terse and not softened by her customary use of the words "my lord." David seemed to be aware of her curtness, because for a second or two, there was a hard, stony look in his eyes. But as quickly as the anger came, it disappeared. His voice, when he spoke, was almost wheedling. "And do you think Yahweh would have given you the words of your song if He hadn't known what I planned? Would there be any need for Him to protect us from the uncircumcised if we stay here in the land of our fathers?"

"I — I don't know," she stammered. "I — this is all so unexpected, my lord. I've been taught all my life to hate the Philistines. To live among them would — would make my flesh crawl."

"And mine, too, I suppose," David agreed. "But if we stay here, Saul will hunt me down like a jackal in the desert. So, would you prefer to have me alive in the household of Achish or dead at the hands of the Lord's anointed?"

He had given her an impossible choice. "But wouldn't Achish kill you as soon as you crossed over into his land?" she asked weakly.

David smiled. "Not if I do it right. Is there anything to prevent stories reaching Achish before we do? Stories that will say I am hunted and hated by Saul — and that I wish to return the hatred? Stories that will declare my willingness to turn against my own people? Stories that will arouse Achish's sympathy toward me and make him look on me as one more weapon to use against the Israelites?"

"But the stories wouldn't be true, my lord."

David laughed. "You and I know that; Achish would not."

For a long time she didn't answer. She sat and met David's

bright stare with a searching gaze. And slowly the conviction grew in her that although David was plotting a deceitful action, it would not be an act of deceit against his own people or his own God. As clearly as though David had outlined his ideas, she saw what he planned to do.

When she finally spoke, her voice had lost its tremulous tone of shock and disapproval. "You plan, then, to simply *pretend* an affection for the Philistines? In actuality, you plan to somehow maintain a good relationship with your own people?"

David nodded with satisfaction. "I thought you'd grasp the idea. Your mind is so keen that I was sure you'd understand. For example, when I go out to do battle, what is there to prevent my telling Achish that I am raiding the Israelites when, actually, I'll be raiding the tribes south of Judah, such as the Amalekites? Then I'll share the spoils with my own people, which ought to do much to ensure their affection for me."

"But what if word of that should get back to Achish?" she asked.

"How can word get back?" David asked, his voice suddenly grim and cold. "If every man, woman, and child is killed on our raids, how can word get back?"

She felt hot and faint. "I thought you — you hated the killing," she said.

"I am going to be king of Israel," David said in so hard a voice that she hardly recognized it. "I don't care what I have to do, short of harming Saul or any member of his family. You, of all people, should understand."

"I just never thought — I never guessed it would require something like this, my lord," she said.

"Well, now you know. I expect your support. You can do a lot to prepare the women so that they don't wail and pull back on their men."

It was on the tip of her tongue to protest that they would all be living a lie and that Yahweh had commanded His people not to lie. But she didn't say it. She had known for years, hadn't she, that David would be king? She had known it from Samuel's words, from her own dreams, from the way Yahweh had put words of prophecy in her mouth. So what right did she have now to protest the means, even though she might always regret them?

"I will do anything my lord commands me," she said, unable to keep the sullenness out of her voice.

But David was too intent on his own ideas to even hear it. "I have a dozen plans," he confided. "I have spies chosen who will prepare the way for us. We'll start out in a day or two, but we'll go by a circuitous route. I plan to pay short visits to as many villages as possible — to as many tribes. I want all of Israel, or at least the southern tribes, to know that David is not deserting them — that he is only escaping the madness of Saul.

"I want to stop in Hebron," he added suddenly. "Would you like to visit your parents for a day or two?"

Delight struggled with suspicion in her mind. Was he, by any chance, bribing her, too? Was part of the charm and warmth he showed toward her simply a means of gaining her devotion?

"My lord knows that I would be happy to visit my parents." But she did not run to him and fling her arms around him as she would have done yesterday.

"You don't *act* happy," he said.

"My lord, I am not a child to persuade from its grief by dangling a toy in front of its eyes."

Unexpectedly, David laughed. "No, you're not, are you," he said. "But I wasn't looking for a child when I fell in love with a woman arrogant enough to defy her husband and bring food to an outlaw."

She trembled with weakness. It had been so easy to fight Nabal's harshness; it was nearly impossible to fight David's magnetism.

"Tomorrow I'll talk to Joab," David said, "and make my final plans. He'll only say 'I told you so' if I suggest you aren't cooperative. He didn't approve my coming to you first, you know."

"Joab doesn't care for me," she said.

"What does it matter? *I* care for you."

He was smiling at her, and she felt her mouth turn up in a responsive smile even though she had not willed it so. *But who could resist him*, she thought, looking at his golden beauty, feeling, oddly enough, a brief spasm of sympathy for the king of the Philistines.

16

DURING THE FEW DAYS they were in Hebron, Abigail saw David very little. He and his followers made camp outside the city, and his time was devoted to talk with the men of the village. He came one night to dinner in Eliab's house, but beyond a look, a touch, an endearing word or two, he acted as though he didn't even know Abigail.

I'll have to get used to this, she thought as she helped her mother serve steaming bowls of lentils and baskets of hot bread to the men. *My time with David, my precious time, was at En Gedi. Even in Philistia he will be too busy with the affairs of men to talk to me. I wish we were back in the cave, even with its damp floor and smoky fire.*

When the men were all served, Abigail, Zopporah, and Rachel sat together outside the kitchen to eat. After a few minutes of casual conversation, Zopporah asked, "And is it true what your father tells me — that you are heading for the land of the Philistines?"

Abigail and Rachel exchanged a swift glance. They had had very little time to discuss the situation, but Abigail knew that Rachel shared her apprehension.

"It's not to be told to just anyone, Mother," Abigail warned.

"Am I just anyone, then?" Zopporah asked indignantly.

"No, of course not. But you know what I mean."

Zopporah shook her head. "It's wicked to go beyond the boundaries of the land of Yahweh."

"Mother!" The old indignation at her mother's apparent obtuseness colored Abigail's voice. "If we go to the land of the Philistines, Yahweh will be there with us. He's not limited to a single place as our Father Abraham thought."

"Perhaps not," Zopporah said stubbornly, "but there are evil gods and goddesses in Philistia. They are unclean and will defile the followers of Yahweh if they are even looked at."

"Then we won't look at them," Abigail said.

"And how are you going to prevent it? If you live in houses beside the Philistines, if you walk past their temples, if you trade in their markets, how do you propose to prevent it?"

Abigail and Rachel exchanged glances again. There was, unfortunately, so much truth in what Zopporah was saying that to disregard her would be silly.

"I don't know, Mother," Abigail admitted. "I don't know what my lord David plans to do."

"It may be that he hasn't even thought of it," Zopporah said. "His mind may be so fixed on military and political things that he hasn't thought of the danger of other gods. Perhaps if you went to the priest who follows David — Abiathar — is that his name?"

"Yes, Abiathar." But Abigail did not go on. Her mind was working furiously, sorting through her mother's words, seeing the truth in them, searching for an answer.

"Then why not go to him?" Zopporah insisted.

It was Rachel who answered. "My sister has no need to go to a priest, Mother. She has the ear of David, her husband. I think she could go directly to him."

Although Rachel was speaking to Zopporah, Abigail felt that the words were directed at her.

"Yes," Abigail said. "Rachel's right. I'll talk to David myself. I'll talk to him as soon as I can."

The words were hardly said when Benjamin came toward them. "No, sit," he said as all three women started to get to their feet. "I came to talk a little while to my mother. Rachel, stay with us. But you, Abigail, David wants to talk to you. He's waiting in the dining room."

Abigail felt her heart jolt. She had not expected an opportunity to talk to David so soon, and she hadn't sorted out her jumbled thoughts. She wasn't ready yet. But she thanked her brother for the message and went swiftly to where David waited.

"My lord," she said when she came into the room.

David was alone, and he turned from the window where he had been standing, looking out at the town of Hebron. He said nothing in response to her greeting but simply opened his arms, and she walked into them.

"I've missed you," he said.

"I've missed you, too," she answered.

He didn't even kiss her. He just held her and rested his cheek against her hair as though he were very tired. "I keep remembering the nights when we sat at the fire and played our lyres and sang our songs. I keep wondering if such hours of peace will ever come again."

"I know," she said. "I feel the same. I've been trying to learn to live without you."

For another minute he held her, seeming to find comfort in her closeness. Finally he pulled back a little. "Joab tells me the spies are coming back with assurances that Achish is willing to have us," David said. "He apparently knew all about me and was just waiting for a chance to invite me to come to Gath. I think we can go directly from Hebron."

"I'm sure you're relieved, my lord," she said without expression.

"I was so sure at first," David said. "I confess I'm getting a little uneasy. I don't know why."

She sat on one of the benches and he joined her. "Perhaps you're worried, as I am, that the men might stray from the teachings of Yahweh," she said. "That they might be seduced by the gods of Philistia."

David sighed. "I haven't wanted to face up to it. I wouldn't even talk to Abiathar about it. But, as usual, you force the truth out of me. Yes, I'm worried."

"Is there no way, my lord, to keep our people separated from the Philistines? No way to make sure that we wouldn't be exposed to their ways? If we could build our own place to stay, that would be the answer, wouldn't it?"

"I think Achish is already thinking of our arrival as a visit from someone who will be extremely valuable to him. His sympathies have been with me for a long time, I'm told. If he could be persuaded that we need a city of our own, a walled city that would be already built — and would keep us safe?"

She did not smile. "You're too clever, my lord. No one is safe from your persuasion. Achish will give you your heart's desire. You will even have him believing he's doing himself a favor."

David laughed. "You make it sound like a crime. Why do you think Yahweh made me 'persuasive,' as you put it? He must have had a reason, and I think it's this: If I'm to be king — if somehow, and only Yahweh knows how — the people of all of Israel are to proclaim me king someday, then I must be a man who can win and hold loyalty."

"I suppose so," she said. "I wish — I wish it could all be done openly and honestly from the beginning."

"Well, it can't, so don't fret about it. Now, what I really wanted to see you about was to ask if you've taken the time to visit the women at the camp."

"Of course, my lord. Wasn't that a duty of mine?"

He nodded. "I just thought you might have found it difficult to leave your mother. Well, anyway, I'm anxious to know that all is well. Is Ahinoam all right? The traveling isn't harmful for the child she carries, is it?"

She was too honest to delude herself about the pain she felt. It was jealousy and nothing else.

"Everyone is fine, my lord. Ahinoam is here in my parents' house most of the time. Today she has gone to my aunt's house to rest because it's quieter there. She's well and not too unhappy, my lord. Like most of the women, she's worried about this move."

"Then you'll have to reassure her," David said. "I don't want the child carried by a woman who is sad and frightened. It's the child I'm worried about. My first child naturally concerns me."

"Of course, my lord." Her voice was stiff.

He spoke wearily. "Look, Abigail, I wish it were you carrying the child — not Ahinoam. You're smart enough to know that. Don't make things any harder for me than they already are."

She flushed with unexpected shame. "I'm sorry," she said. "I'll look out for Ahinoam more than I have. She — she likes me, I think. By the time we get to Philistia, I'll try to have her believing that it's the will of Yahweh that her child be born in foreign places."

"And for all we know, it is," David responded. "I'll count on you, then, to see that she is safe and happy — or as happy as possible."

"Yes, my lord."

He hesitated. "I wish I didn't have to go back to the men. I wish that we could sit together on the roof of your father's house and make a song. I wish that even for a few days, we could think only of each other."

"I wish so, too, my lord. But I don't think there will ever again come a time when we're free to think only of each other."

"Yes, there will. When we're settled in the kingdom of Achish, before spring comes when we'll have to go out to fight, surely there will be nights when we can sit by a fire and talk and sing again."

"I hope so, my lord."

"And make a child," he said.

"I live for such a hope," she admitted.

"Then it's settled." His voice was certain, almost merry. "Now, I must get back — and you must wait, as I will, for the time in Philistia when we can be together again."

His kiss was warm, but she felt that his mind had already drifted to the plans that had to be made and carried out. He had little need for her now, she thought, except to look out for Ahinoam. Well, at least she had planted the idea of a separate city for the Israelites in David's mind. But surely Yahweh expected her to do greater things than this.

"How can you be so calm about it? Aren't you afraid, as I am, that the Philistines will butcher us all as soon as we enter their land?"

Abigail looked at Ahinoam's worried face and felt an unexpected twist of pity in her heart. "No, my sister," she said. "And I'm not as calm as you think. I'm a woman just as you are. But I believe our lord knows exactly what he's doing."

"You're not carrying a child to worry about," Ahinoam said, folding her hands across the front of her body protectively. "Not that I mean to boast of my own condition," she added apologetically. "You know I don't —"

"I know, I know. You'll share my joy when I conceive. I know that."

"It's just — it's just that I think about a baby born in a foreign country, with foreign gods all around, and everything different from home."

Her eyes filled with tears as she gazed sadly at Abigail.

"But if we had stayed in the caves at En Gedi," Abigail argued, "you'd have felt as though you were home, wouldn't you?"

"Well, of course. I —"

"Then what makes a home? It's the people around you; it's knowing that Yahweh is with you; it's doing the things you've done all your life. It will be like that, I promise you, my sister. Our lord is concerned about your sadness and your worry. For his sake, can't you try to be brave?"

"Is he really concerned?"

Abigail saw the joy on the girl's face. *She may not be jealous,* Abigail thought with a sense of revelation, *because it's not her nature to be jealous. That doesn't mean she doesn't love David.*

"Yes, he spoke about it to me yesterday at my father's house," Abigail said gently. "He has a hundred things to worry about, a thousand details to see to. You won't add to his burden by being frightened, will you? I promise I'll take care of you — of you and the child."

Ahinoam tried to smile. "Then I won't fret any more," she promised. "I just wish I knew how to be brave."

"Ask Yahweh for courage," Abigail said. "And before we leave Hebron, talk to my mother about how Yahweh has given her faith. She's very wise."

"I'm sorry I'm such a bother," Ahinoam apologized. "But —"

Abigail stood up abruptly, suddenly tired of her role of comforter. "It's all right," she said. "You're no bother. Our greatest concern is for the child, so how can you be a bother? Come now and talk to my mother. I think she's kneading bread in the yard. She'll be glad for company. Rachel is with her, I think."

"Will you come, too, my sister?"

"No, I'm going to walk to the end of that distant field. It's nearly time for my father to come home. I want to meet him."

She didn't tell Ahinoam — she wouldn't be able to admit to anyone — that the reason she wanted to meet Eliab was because she, too, was afraid. In spite of all of David's reassurances, she needed to feel, one more time, the sense of her father's protective love. She wanted to know, for just an hour or two, the sensation of being a child again in a child's carefree world.

17

THE BRIGHT SPRING SUN made patches of light on the stone floor of the house that still seemed like a stranger's house to Abigail, even though it had been home to David's household for more than a year. Abigail stood by the window, staring out at the landscape, tallying the things about this place that distressed her. *Even the winter rains had been different here in Philistia,* she thought. A year and a half ago, when the rains had come sweeping across the wilderness, shutting her and David into the warmth and privacy of the cave at En Gedi, she had been refreshed and exhilarated by the clean power of the storm. But here in the Philistine city of Ziklag, the winter rains had come shrouded with mist and fog, carrying the salt smell of the sea. And now, even though it was their second spring in the city which the Philistine king had given them, she still found the sudden burgeoning of trees and shrubs too lush. There was a softness here that lay heavily over the heart.

"Is my sister busy?"

Abigail turned toward Ahinoam and found herself smiling involuntarily. The little boy in Ahinoam's arms was so beautiful, so much like David, that no one could resist him.

"Never too busy for you and little Amnon." Abigail moved toward the two in the doorway, holding out her hands, and Amnon almost fell out of his mother's arms reaching for her.

"I think he prefers you to me," Ahinoam said in her sweet, colorless voice.

"Nonsense! He merely enjoys being held on such a large stomach," Abigail said, laughing. "His little brother is warm and kicking, yet takes no attention from him. Or his little sister," she added hastily.

Ahinoam laughed lightly and lifted her hand to brush back the baby's hair. "A brother, I hope," she murmured. "If our lord is indeed to be a king, he will need sons to succeed him."

The quick glitter of stones set in a circle of silver caught Abigail's eyes. Ahinoam had not had that bracelet before. It must be part of the spoils that David had brought back from one of his constant raids. Why would he give gifts to Ahinoam when he still had not started going to her room? Or had he? When he had told Abigail he was working on plans with Joab, had he gone to Ahinoam?

Abigail buried her face against Amnon's curls, hoping Ahinoam would not see any indication of the pain and anger that blazed inside her. She had no right to the anger, of course. She had known that from the very beginning. The pain was her own affair.

"Whether it's a boy or girl is in Yahweh's hands," Abigail said, trying to hold her voice steady.

Ammon spied his mother's bracelet and reached for it with a squeal of delight.

"No," Ahinoam said. "You mustn't touch. Our lord gave it to me," she said innocently to Abigail. "I think he did it to ease his feelings of obligation to me. He — he never comes to lie with me. He gives me gifts instead."

Abigail felt almost faint with the sweet rush of relief that poured over her. "He will surely come," she said, and knew that the sound of promise in her voice was not sincere. "When my child is born, when our lord is lonely at night during my period of uncleanliness, he'll surely come. The purpose of wives is to provide sons."

She was saying the words as much to herself as to Ahinoam. But the tall girl, still standing in the doorway, shook her head with soft stubbornness. "Our lord is sentimental, my sister. He is a poet who dreams of things I cannot share. I don't want him to be king," she said sadly. "I don't have any desire to live in a fine house and watch my son grow up surrounded by people who hate him and yet fawn over him."

It was the most serious thing Abigail had ever heard Ahinoam say. She had obviously done some thinking as she lay alone night after night.

"Your son is the firstborn," Abigail said, amazed as she always was that her jealousy did not spill over onto the child she held in her arms.

"But our lord will prefer *your* child," Ahinoam said in a voice so controlled that Abigail sensed the pain behind it.

"Not if it's a girl," Abigail said, trying to smile. "Or if it should be a boy — but unfit in some way to succeed our lord as king."

"Don't say such things," Ahinoam cried. "You shouldn't even think such things."

"I lost my first baby, remember." But Abigail was moved to guilt by Ahinoam's words.

"That was Nabal's child. This one is David's."

Abigail made no effort to answer the simple faith of Ahinoam's statement. Who knew better than she the difference between the two men?

"Let's take Amnon down into the yard," she said. "We can put him down and let him play. It won't hurt him to be on the grass."

"It will hurt me," Ahinoam confessed. "It hurts my heart. I don't like this city or this land. I want to go home."

Holding Amnon close to the bulk of her own unborn child, Abigail started toward the shallow steps that led to the common room. She wanted to say, "I don't like them, either. I want to go home, too." But someone had to at least make a pretense of being content.

In the elegant house of Achish, lamplight, soft and wavering, cast shifting designs of gold and black on the dark table top. For long moments, the men who sat around the table seemed to be fascinated with the moving play of shadows.

Finally, Achish, who sat at the head of the table, looked up and spoke directly at David.

"But you've known, my son," he said. "You've known that someday Saul would meet us in battle. Why do you act so surprised?"

David traced a circle of light with his finger before he answered. "Did I act surprised, my lord? I didn't intend it to be surprise — unless it would be surprise at your cunning."

Joab, across the table from David, was silent, but at David's words, a quick flicker of relief touched his face so that he was careful not to look at Achish.

"At my cunning?"

"Truly, my lord," David assured him, raising his eyes to look into the face of the king of Philistia. "In all my raids, I had never thought of your scheme of luring all of Israel's army — king, princes, soldiers, all — into so rough a terrain for battle. I think I, myself, would be afraid of ambush."

"Nonsense. Nothing frightens you. Not the fiercest tribes of Judah or Israel. I've seen you come back from raid after raid — laden down with spoils — hardly missing a man."

"Nevertheless," David insisted, "this trick of yours surpasses anything I have ever thought of. How long do you think it will take — to lure them all to the area of Mount Gilboa?"

Achish shrugged. "Who knows? A month. Two or three. My army won't go out until the time is right. But you, my son, will you go with us? Can I tell my captains that David of Bethlehem will be our ally on that day?"

David's eyes continued to meet Achish's. "My lord, I am your slave. If you call me into battle, I am yours to command."

"And, our god, Dagon, will lead us forth." Achish spoke with calm assurance.

"Yes, my lord," David said, "the god, Dagon, will lead you forth."

David shuddered as though there were flies on his skin. "The name of Dagon tasted foul in my mouth," he confessed.

"Yahweh knows you said it only to pacify an old fool," Joab said.

David shot back, "Achish is not a fool. He's shrewder than I wish he were. As to what Yahweh thinks, how can you know? I don't know. I feel as though He were as lost to me as Saul is."

"My lord, you mustn't say things like that."

"It's true, though," David said. "When we watched the sheep under the stars at Bethlehem — when we lived in the caves at En Gedi — Yahweh was as close to me as — as my breath. In this place, He is a stranger."

"But who do you think gives you the victories when you go out on raids?" Joab asked.

"If it's Yahweh," David said, "then why can't He protect me from this dilemma? How can I go to fight against the Lord's anointed? How can I bear it to see the swords of my men — of my own hands — raised against Jonathan?"

"Samuel said you would be king," Joab said. "He never said how it would be achieved."

"I'm sick of it all," David cried. "I'm sick to death of plotting and scheming and killing."

"Would my lord go back into the wilderness? Back into the caves? Would he give up forever the gratitude and adoration of the people of Judah who have taken our gifts of spoil and called down blessings from heaven on the beloved — on David? Would you give it up, my lord, because your hands are a little soiled with blood?"

David met Joab's stare for a long moment. His shoulders sagged with a sudden indication of defeat. "Go away," he whispered. "I don't want to hear your voice any longer."

Joab inclined his head and left, but his eyes were no longer worried, and his mouth was turned up with a small smile of triumph.

Abigail lifted her head to look at David. He had been silent since dinner, striding from one end of the common room to the other, obviously troubled. He had asked Ahinoam to take Amnon away, claiming that the baby's chattering, which usually delighted him, was annoying. Without a word, Ahinoam had lifted the child and left the room. Abigail stood uncertainly for a moment, but the mute command of David's hand had sent her to a chair near the brazier. There she had remained, twisting the thread of a small hand spindle, depending more on touch than sight, since evening dimmed the windows and shadows filled the corners of the room.

David, suddenly halting in mid-stride, asked, "Will you sing for me if I go to get your lyre?"

"Of course, my lord." She laid down the spindle. "You won't have to go anywhere. It's there, see, in the corner."

She started to get up, but David's hand pressed her shoulder and held her in the chair. "I'll get it," he said.

With the lyre balanced against her swollen body and steadied between her hands, she looked up with question. "Any particular song, my lord?"

He kept his head turned away from her. "No, you choose."

She bent her head over the lyre, running her fingers lightly across the strings. *It must be one of David's own songs,* she thought, and chose one at random.

"O Lord, my God," she began, "in Thee I have taken
   refuge;
Save me from all those who pursue me, and deliver me,
Lest he tear my soul like a lion,
Dragging me away while there is none to deliver.

O Lord, my God, if I have done this,
If there is injustice on my hands,
If I have rewarded evil to my friend.
Or have plundered him who without cause was my
    adversary,
Let the enemy pursue my soul and overtake it;
And let him trample my life down to the ground,
And lay my glory in the dust."
David stood very still, the glow from the brazier lighting
his face so that she was reminded of the first night he had
come to her in the cave. "How do you know?" he said.
"How do you always know?"

"Know what, my lord?"

"That I am shamed and heavy with guilt. That I have said
the abominable name of a heathen god. That I have all but
agreed to take up the sword against Saul and Jonathan."

She felt her breath catch in shock, and a strange jagged
pain cut through her head. "My lord, you didn't," she
whispered.

"It was only a cunning pretense at first," he said. "I
thought I was too clever to ever be forced into a corner by
that fox, Achish."

She listened in silence, fear growing in her.

"I'm so tired of bending the knee," David went on in a
hot, furious voice. "I'm weary to death of playing the fool
for Achish. I'd like to — to —" His words broke off with a
gasp of pain. "I will not bear the sword against the Lord's
anointed," he shouted. "It doesn't matter what deceit I
have to practice."

Her hands moved again on the strings, and a low music
crept through the room. "Listen, my lord," she said. "Listen
to the words you sang at En Gedi.

"I will give thanks to the Lord with all my heart;
I will tell of all Thy wonders.
I will be glad and exult in Thee,
I will sing praise to Thy name, O most High."

David's voice, bitter and frustrated, interrupted. "It was

easy to sing such high thoughts in En Gedi. It's different here, with the enemy around me."

"But we had enemies at En Gedi, my lord," she said earnestly. "Wild animals. The armies of Saul."

"But I had Yahweh at my back," David said.

"Surely you have Him still, my lord?"

"Do you?" he asked.

The glib, facile words that rushed into her mind faltered before they reached her lips. If she truly had Yahweh beside her, would she be jealous of Ahinoam — that innocent girl? Would she be waking at night in an agony of fear that the child she carried might be born dead? Would she wake each morning with the desperate feeling that this exile would never end?

"I don't know, my lord," she admitted.

"Even Abiathar doesn't know," David said. "A priest ought to know. Samuel knew."

Samuel. Her thoughts flew back to the day the old man had touched her head in blessing. But Samuel had never had to live in a foreign land. Samuel had never had to face the threat that unless he went to war against his own people, he would be branded a traitor and killed.

"My lord," she began, reaching for the words of assurance that she wanted and that David needed, "listen to me."

The pain came without warning — no slight, hesitant twinge such as heralded the beginning of labor for the first child, but a wrenching, tearing thing that bent her over, gasping for breath.

"Is it the child?" David asked in alarm.

"Yes, the child," she said when she could breathe again. "Have them call the midwife, my lord. This is nothing like the first time. This —"

But David had gone, running from the unknown terrors of childbirth, gone without the comfort she ought to have given him. And she was left alone to face the pain of giving birth and to weep over the pain of her inadequacy.

18

"IT'S A BOY," the midwife said.

Abigail heard the thin, shrill wail. Oh, surely, it was a stronger sound than the first baby's cry. But she was afraid to hope. She licked her dry, bitten lips cautiously and tried out her voice.

"Is he all right?"

The midwife's voice was brisk and matter-of-fact. "He's fine. A little smaller than some but bigger than others. Wait. I'll rub the oil and salt on him and then let you see him." There was a short silence, and when the baby cried again, the midwife's voice came in a complaining grumble. "If your mother hadn't insisted that no one else be here, I'd be able to take care of her instead of you. Don't kick so."

Abigail hadn't wanted anyone else to be in the room. If the child were to be too frail — or even stillborn — she wanted no one else to see her shame — not even Rachel or Topeleth.

But the baby's cry was lusty and strong. Abigail lifted her head to try to see the tiny, squirming body in the midwife's hands.

"Is he all right, *really?*"

The midwife turned at last, the child wrapped with the cloth provided for it. "Here," she said, smiling. "See for yourself. Just because you lost one baby doesn't mean you'll lose all of them. Here, look at him."

She lay the baby on Abigail's chest and then bent to her task of repairing any damage caused by the birth. Caught up in the miracle of the moment, Abigail forgot the pain of the past hours. She was not even aware of what the midwife was doing. There was only this child, whole and perfect and squalling with protest at the indignity of birth.

He wasn't like Amnon at all. Amnon was exactly like David. This child was like Eliab and Benjamin — dark, strong-chinned, with a full, wide mouth.

"May I put him to the breast?" she asked.

"You can try," the midwife said. "Sometimes they aren't much interested."

Almost fearfully, Abigail shifted the baby. Her memory of the first baby's feeble attempt at nursing was strong in her mind. But this boy was truly different, she realized with a sense of exultation. He nuzzled against her and began to nurse as though he had done it a dozen times before.

The midwife glanced up and chuckled. "No one has to teach that one, hm? There! You're all right. And so is the boy. Now, may I send Ahinoam in?"

Abigail never took her eyes from the tiny face puckered with concentration. "Yes, send her in," she murmured.

Ahinoam was plainly delighted. "I've been so worried," she said. "You should have let me be with you. my sister. It's been terrible—just waiting. Ah, let me see him. Amnon didn't nurse that strongly so soon after birth. What a man you have!"

Abigail smiled. "He doesn't look like our lord the way Amnon does. But he's alive. He's strong."

"What name are you going to give him?" Ahinoam asked, running a gentle fingertip along the baby's head. "Have you and my lord decided?"

Exhaustion swept over Abigail with surprising suddenness. "I don't know," she whispered. "Chileab, I think."

"It seems a strange name for a king's son," Ahinoam said.

"By the time our lord is king," Abigail said drowsily, "it will seem right."

She was only dimly aware of Ahinoam's taking the baby from her breast, settling him down beside Abigail, and then turning to leave the room.

"Sleep, my sister," she said.

But Abigail did not need the admonition. She was already asleep.

She woke suddenly with a start, sure that she had rolled over and crushed the baby. The room was dim with the coming on of night, but there was enough light from the small, flickering lamp for her to see the baby lying safely beside her. She raised herself on an elbow and leaned over him, listening for the sound of his breathing. Faint and rapid, the small sound was like music to her. Her hand curved around the little body and held it close for a minute. Then she released the possessive clutch of her fingers and lay back to look at her son.

"Will my lord find you fair?" she whispered, and it was like the line of a song. "Will he make you a prince in his house?"

The fragile sound of the breathing went on calmly, undisturbed by her whispered words. Abigail smoothed her finger along his cheek.

"I don't want you to be a prince," she whispered, amazed at herself. "Ahinoam was right. There will be too much pain in it — in being David's son. Poor little boy — to be the child of a man who has been chosen by God."

Topeleth came through the door. "You're awake," she said. "I've been in twice to admire your son, but you never heard me. I'm glad you're awake now. I wouldn't want you to wake up and find him gone."

"What do you mean — gone?" Abigail asked anxiously.

"Why, gone to see his father, of course." Topeleth spoke with amusement. "Our lord is back from his latest raid, and he has heard the news with joy. He's eager to see his son."

"Then take him," Abigail said, astonished to find, as soon as Topeleth carried the baby away, that her arms felt empty, so quickly had Chileab become essential to her. She wondered now how she had endured the loss of the first child.

Yahweh was with me, she remembered with gratitude. *Just as He was with my mother. Perhaps He is closer to women when they have just borne a child.* She lay smiling.

"So you gave me a son?" The voice was David's, and she turned her head to see him standing beyond the threshold of the door, the baby held in his arms.

"Have I pleased you, my lord?"

"Do you have to ask?"

"No, my lord. It was a woman's question. I know that Yahweh has allowed me to please you."

He grinned at her. "A fine boy. Like your family, and that's good. One Bethlehemite in this household is fine — now, a small Calebite will be an added treasure."

"Would you love him, my lord, if he were not fit and strong? If, for some reason, he could never be a true prince?"

David frowned at her. "What nonsense is that? The boy is perfect — fit, in every way, to be the son of a king."

"But if he weren't, my lord?" she persisted, not at all sure why she was asking the question.

David stared at her from across the room. "I wish I were allowed to come close to you," he muttered. "I'd like to shake a little sense into your head — gently, of course."

"Yes, my lord." She tried to smile but did not take her eyes from his.

"Yes," David said at last, the word abrupt and impatient. "I would love him in any way — perfect or imperfect. He's my son. Yours and mine. Do you think I'm a monster?"

"I think you are — the beloved," she said daringly. "Beloved of Yahweh and of the people of Judah. Beloved of — of your son's mother."

David's eyes were somber. "You choose a bad time to tell me, my love. For a year and a half I've been trying to get you to say you love me. Now you choose to tell me on the night when I have promised I will go to Ahinoam's room."

Breathless from the pain that impaled her, she only lay and stared at the man who held her son in his arms and her life in his hands. "I've — I've been expecting it, my lord," she gasped.

"The first night," David reminded her. "The very first night I came to you, we talked about it — about a king's responsibilities. You seemed to understand. I haven't gone before, because I couldn't even think of sleeping without you beside me. But since you can't lie beside me for weeks, I thought this might be the time —"

"Of course, my lord. I told Ahinoam several weeks ago that I thought this was when you'd come to her."

"You did?"

"Truly, my lord."

"Abigail, I can't bear to sleep alone. Achish will be going forth to battle against Saul in about a month. My waking and sleeping hours are haunted with horror. Can you understand?"

With a courage she did not know she possessed, she dredged up the grace to say gently, "Of course. I know that what love you share with my sister will not make you care less for me."

He moved restlessly. "Less? Don't be silly. You can't even guess how much I'll be longing for you."

The baby started to cry, fretfully and shrilly. "He's hungry," David said, looking down into Chileab's face. "I'll take him to Topeleth so that he can be brought to you." He turned away, then turned back to her. "Thank you for my son," he said softly. "You are dearer to me than I can say."

He turned and strode away. When Topeleth brought the baby in, she found Abigail dry-eyed and calm. With much bustling and many crooning words, the old woman settled the baby in the crook of Abigail's arm and saw to it that he began to suck noisily.

"What a baby!" she said admiringly. "He makes up for all the sorrow over the one we didn't keep."

Abigail tried to smile. "You've been faithful and good,

and I'm grateful. Since things are different here —'' Her voice failed, and she knew that if she tried to form more words, she would weep. She bent her head to look at the baby.

Topeleth put her hand to Abigail's shoulder. "It's all right," she said. "Better to be with you and your lord in a cave than to stay with my nephew's greedy son. Listen, Abigail, I know that our lord will go to Ahinoam tonight. I heard him tell her so. If it grieves you, you needn't be ashamed."

Abigail took a deep breath. "I will not weep and give my son bitterness for milk. I will not!" She clenched her teeth against the ache in her throat.

"Then, when he has fed," Topeleth said as calmly as though she were discussing a method of making bread. "And when you have laid him beside you, then you'll be free to weep. I won't let anyone come into your room."

She knelt, laboriously, and kissed Abigail's cheek. "Yahweh never promised us that life would always be lovely," she said softly. "Accept the mercy of tears, little one. They're a gift from Yahweh, too."

She got up as laboriously as she had knelt and without a backward look, left the room.

Abigail fed her child without movement or sound. If she tried to say anything, she knew her rigid composure would shatter. She concentrated on the child at her breast, memorizing the sight and feel and smell of him. When he fell asleep, she put him gently down on the mat.

Then, finally, she let herself think of Topeleth's words. "Accept the mercy of tears," she had said. "They're a gift from Yahweh, too."

Despite all the humiliation and pain she had endured in Nabal's house, she had rarely wept. But now, with Topeleth's words to guide her, she allowed all her grief and fear and frustration to well up into a paroxysm of weeping that nearly shook her apart.

It wasn't only jealousy that David was going to Ahinoam,

she knew. It was a dread of the future that she had never really admitted to herself before. Now that David had gone away from her for even one night, it would never again be her privilege to simply assume that he would share her bed. For a long time she wept, but gradually her tears slowed and stopped.

"Oh, Yahweh, help me," she whispered thickly, "help me through this night."

The windows were full dark when Topeleth came into the room with warm water in a basin and a small container of hot broth. Without comment, the older woman bathed Abigail's face and brushed her hair. Then, gently, lovingly, she spooned the nourishing broth into Abigail's mouth. When her ministrations were finished, she spoke briskly. "Tomorrow you will start to get up. You may be confined to this room for seven days, but that won't keep you from taking care of your baby — and playing your lyre and being happy."

Abigail didn't answer, and Topeleth went on sternly. "You had a husband once who treated you with contempt. You bore a son who died. Then Yahweh brought you to a man who loved you. And you have a living, strong son. Can't you endure the rest?"

"I'm not as brave as I thought I was," Abigail confessed.

"Then ask Yahweh for more courage," Topeleth said. "You had a right to weep in sorrow, but now you have to turn away from grief."

Abigail nodded. "Thank you," she managed to say. "You're good to me."

"As Yahweh would have me be," Topeleth said simply, and set about putting the room in order.

Yahweh's goodness does not always come in dreams or music or stars, Abigail reflected soberly. *Sometimes it comes in the simple kindness of an old woman.*

By the time Topeleth left, the house was completely silent,

as a house is when everyone is asleep. Topeleth's presence had kept Abigail from hearing the murmur of David's and Ahinoam's voices.

Well, then, my prayer was answered, Abigail realized with a sense of wonder. *I asked for help to endure this night, and it was given to me. If Yahweh can bless* me, *surely He will not overlook His servant David.*

Certainty and peace flowed into her heart and filled it to overflowing. Never before had she been so sure that her God answered prayer. Her jealousy was a small thing compared to the danger of David's situation. But Yahweh had met *her* need, and she had no doubt of His power to work whatever miracle David required.

19

THE DAYS SLIPPED BY. Released from her ritual isolation after seven days, Abigail took up her usual role in the household. Except for the fact that David did not come to her room — could not, in fact, come with propriety for thirty-three days — things might have been as they had always been. As long as Abigail did not go near the room set aside for worship, as long as she did not touch any holy thing, there was no longer any stigma attached to her person, and David was free to sit with her, to touch her with gentleness and even, at times, with a thinly veiled desire. He did not, Abigail saw with some degree of comfort, go to Ahinoam's room every night. Sometimes, he slept on a mat in the common room or sat up half the night, making plans with Joab.

Not that any of the plans seemed to hold any promise, he confided one night to Abigail.

"I've tried every trick I know," David admitted. "I've come up with a dozen possible means of escaping this abomination, but none of them are practical. None of them will work."

"Have you prayed, my lord?"

"That's an idiotic question. Of course I've prayed. Would I attempt anything without seeking Yahweh's aid first?"

"It's not enough just to ask Him what to do." Her voice was strangely authoritative, not the voice of a submissive wife at all. "You have to have faith that Yahweh *can* save you from the situation."

He stared at her in astonishment. "Do you think you're Samuel to know what I should do?"

"My lord, I *know* that Yahweh can save you. I'm positive a miracle will happen."

Before she could say any more, Chileab began to cry in the next room.

"Why is he crying?" David demanded.

"It's time to feed him, my lord."

David did not smile. "Then feed him. When you're finished, come and we'll talk again."

But half an hour later when she hurried back to the common room, David was deep in conference with Joab, so there was nothing for her to do but go to her own bed. And before morning broke, messengers from Achish were hammering on the door, calling David to join his men with the soldiers of Philistia and ride against Saul and Jonathan.

The flurry and chaos of the departure left little or no time for proper farewells. David held his sons briefly, blessed them with a kiss, touched his lips to Ahinoam's cheek, and allowed himself a fierce kiss on Abigail's mouth. Then he was gone.

For a little while, the women stood dazed and unbelieving. The threat had been held at bay by inaction and their own hope for so long that they had almost come to believe it would never happen.

"What will we do?" Rachel said. "We can't just stand here, can we? Shouldn't we make some kind of plan? Do something?"

"Call the women together," Abigail said after a minute of silent thought. "We can discuss some possibilities and then get to work. There are always tasks to fill our hours. We don't have to sit empty-handed and empty-hearted unless we choose to."

"Come, Ahinoam," Rachel said. "Let's go from house to

house and tell the women to gather here at our lord David's house." She thrust her little girl, born several months before Chileab, into Abigail's arms. "Watch her, my sister,'" she added, and it was a mark of her growing confidence that she didn't even add the word "please."

Abigail cuddled the little girl against her and reached down her hand to Amnon. He grabbed her finger and toddled along beside her as she made her way toward the common room. Suddenly he pulled away from her and ran toward a clod of dirt on the ground. She snatched him away from it and he wailed lustily, slapping at her hands in temper.

"Do you think, young man," she said with quick fury, "that you're going to get everything you want — just because you want it? Just because your father will be king?"

The words stopped Amnon's crying because she so rarely spoke crossly to him. He stared at her, his eyes big with wonder, shoving his thumb into his mouth for comfort. Abigail, herself, was also halted by her words. How could she be so sure, even now, that David would be king? And yet, the conviction grew until she was again warm with certainty. She had no idea *how* the thought could be put into Achish's head that David should be sent back to Ziklag. But she was sure, beyond doubt, that Yahweh would find a way.

The women and children of David's army crowded into the common room of David's house. They spilled out into the courtyard, and the sound of children crying or laughing wove a shrill counterpart to the distressed murmur of women's voices. *Why do I hear a song even in this moment of agony,* Abigail thought. *Well, it's the way Yahweh made me.*

She pitched her voice so that it would carry to the farthest woman. "It's nothing new for us to be left alone," she said, "with only a few old men to act as sentries and guards. So I know you will not get hysterical and weep at the first strange sound or the coming of nighttime."

Almost miraculously, the women assumed an air of calmness as though to justify her words.

"But it's different this time," Abigail went on. "Our men have been called out to fight our own people. We have to face the fact that things might be — changed — when they come home."

"*If* they come home," one of the women said sullenly.

"The god, Dagon, rode at the head of the army," another woman cried out. "I saw a priest carrying the image. Ought we to pray to him, then?"

Abigail felt a chill of horror along her skin at the use of the god's name in David's house. She was grateful to hear an immediate clamor of protest.

"What a blasphemy!" "We pray only to Yahweh." "The pagan god is evil." "What are you thinking of?"

Abigail let the clamor go on. There was something cleansing in the ability to shout aloud against a pagan god and to proclaim a belief in the Lord God, Yahweh.

But finally, she raised her hands and spoke in a loud, clear voice. "You see then? We are *not* women of Philistia — even though we have lived in this town of Ziklag for eighteen months. We are women of Israel. We are daughters of Yahweh."

"But what if we're spit on by the Israelites because our men have gone forth against Saul? What if we can never go home?"

Abigail searched for words of reassurance. "I'm not sure," she admitted at last. "I've asked you to come here to ask you to pray as you have never prayed before. Pray that Achish will have a change of heart and that he will release David from his obligation. I *know* it's possible."

The women stared and muttered, but one by one, their faces cleared and settled into lines of determination.

"The priest, Abiathar, is not here," one woman called. "How can we worship if there is no priest to lead us?"

"Yahweh will listen. And besides, your children must see only courage in you. They mustn't be filled with our fear."

"Then we'll pray," Topeleth said. "Come, let's go about our tasks, and as we work, we'll pray."

Abigail smiled with gratitude at the older woman. "She's right," she cried. "My aunt is right. Our work will be a sign of devotion and faith."

There was a general chorus of approval, and Abigail spoke out with a sturdy show of strength. "Then let's get busy and work without fear. Are you agreed, my sisters?"

"Agreed," they called, and began to scatter, each to her own house.

"Rachel, stay here with us," Abigail urged. "Tell your girls to come here to our house. I'd feel better if you were here."

Rachel stood staring at Abigail. "You're really afraid, my sister? All the courage was only a pretense?"

"I'm not afraid about David," Abigail said, "but there's something cold that walks on my skin and a heavy weight that sits in my stomach. I don't understand what it is, but I confess I'm afraid."

"Then I'll come," Rachel said. "Let me run over and get some grain and a few things for the baby. Will you keep her here until I come back?"

"Of course. Only hurry."

All over Ziklag, Abigail could hear the soft, floating sound of women's voices, raised in song or in the ordinary sounds of household communication. But over the light cadence of women's voices, there was a dark sound of danger that no one else seemed to hear. Ahinoam, Topeleth, and the serving girls all went competently about their business, heedless of the silent thrumming through the air. But Abigail heard it, and her blood ran cold while her heart thudded against her chest.

By the time Rachel had returned and the rhythm of the work had captured all the women in the house, Abigail began to believe that perhaps it had only been her own fear that had hummed in her ears. She began to relax a little, trying to push her apprehension to the back of her mind.

The afternoon was more than half gone when the sudden, unexpected shout of sentries was heard.

"Is it our lord returning?" Ahinoam cried, starting to run toward the door.

"Wait!" Abigail's voice was sharp. "Wait!"

The cry came again, a loud, frightened cry which was picked up by the terrified women and thrown through the air from house to house, from street to street.

"Amalekites! The Amalekites are coming! And there is no one to save us!"

So this was the unseen horror that had walked like a scorpion across her skin. Abigail stared at Rachel, seeing her own terror reflected in her sister-in-law's face.

"Quick," Abigail shouted. "Every women get her own child. One of you girls run to the next house, and send someone on from house to house. Tell them not to try to save anything except the children. Tell them to step out in their courtyards in a sign of surrender. If we don't defy them, if we don't fight for our belongings, perhaps we'll be spared rape and capture. Hurry!"

The shrieks of horror began to die down, and by the time the crashing of the smashed gates was heard, the town of Ziklag was silent, filled with quiet women and children, waiting for the horde of desert marauders to come thundering down the street that led to the house of David.

part IV

Then it happened...that the
Amalekites...had overthrown
Ziklag and burned it with fire;
and they took captive the women.
...Now David's two wives had
been taken captive, Ahinoam
...and Abigail....But David
pursued....And David slaughtered
them....So David recovered all that
the Amalekites had taken, and
rescued his two wives.

1 Samuel 30:1-2*a*, 5, 10*a*,17*a*, 18

20

A VAST HORDE OF MEN rode down the dusty street toward
Abigail, spurring their camels and yelling with a fierce
mixture of fury and glee. Some of them brandished long,
curling whips, laughing when the women or children
retreated in terror from the cracking tips. Others carried
naked swords which they slashed in whistling arcs through
the air.

The leader, swarthy and dirty, pulled his camel to a stop
beside David's house. His eyes raked over the women
standing in the yard, discarding one after another, finally
coming to rest on Abigail's face.

"Where are your men?" he shouted.

"I don't know," she said coolly.

One of the whips flicked the ground so close to her feet
that dust spurted against her bare ankle. Somehow she kept
from flinching.

"You *do* know. Tell me where they are."

"They don't tell us where they're going," she said, "or
when they're coming back."

The leader howled with laughter, revealing gapped, rotten
teeth. "You can't fool us. We know they're gone with Achish's
army."

"Then why did you ask me?" Her voice was not only
cold, but insolent.

The whip snaked out again, and the flick of the end caught her robe and lifted it to the middle of her thighs.

The leader turned to the man with the whip. "Don't let your skill go to your head. She'll pay for her disrespect when the time comes."

Abigail heard the caught breath of the women behind her, but no one moved.

"What do you want?" Abigail asked. "If it's food or water you're seeking, my women will get it for you."

The leader leered. "Ah, haven't we always heard of the hospitality of the Hebrews? Even their women, unarmed and unprotected, can offer it. Do your women offer a warmer welcome than food and water, my lady?"

The term of respect had slipped out without intention, she was sure, and she saw the quick look of vexation in his eyes.

"My women and I are believers in Yahweh, the Lord our God. We would offer nothing of what you are suggesting, sir."

"You may not be given the choice," another man called out, grinning at his fellows.

Abigail opened her mouth to answer, but Topeleth must have sensed the anger than crowded to Abigail's lips, because the older woman spoke up quickly in a gentle voice. "We are defenseless, my lord. To be taken as spoils by the victor in battle is one thing — but there is no army to fight, my lord. There are only the mothers of Ziklag and their children."

An uneasiness that might almost have been embarrassment flickered in and out of the leader's eyes. Abigail saw one of the men lick his lips with greed. She was almost certain the man was looking at Rachel, but she dared not turn her head to look. Somehow, she must keep eye contact with the leader. Cruel as he appeared, he was obviously in control of his ruffian army.

"We've ridden a long way, Dorfu," one of the men yelled. "Whether we've earned it or not, surely you'll let us seek out a girl we want. You won't deny us that?"

Dorfu met Abigail's eyes steadily for a long, silent moment, without bothering to answer his soldier. Just when she thought she could not bear another second of the hard, level gaze, the man dropped his eyes and turned toward his men.

"Hear me," he shouted. His voice carried back along the rank of men. "Hear me now. If the women are to be enjoyed, it will not be here in this foreign city. We'll take them home — and there we'll divide them — each having his choice. But until we get back to our own village, not a woman is to be touched. Do you understand me?"

There was an angry mutter from some of the men, but Dorfu sat unmoving, glaring at his followers. One by one, they looked away from him, submissive to his command.

Back at the end of the column, a young, strong voice rang out. "We'll wait for the women, Dorfu. But you can't deny us everything we came for. We have a right to plunder the houses."

Dorfu waved an assenting hand. "Help yourselves. Wait! You six here in front — you round up the women and children. Get them together at the gates. No, don't worry — you'll get your share of the spoils. All right, men, take what you want. Then set the torch to every house! But don't touch the women!"

He was looking directly at Abigail when he shouted the last words. As clearly as though he had said the words aloud, she understood what he was thinking. In that way, his eyes said, I will be able to save *you* for *me!*

Clutching Chileab against her breast, Abigail watched the men slide from their camels and start to fan out across the town. The six appointed by Dorfu moved with a ruthless precision that indicated this particular action was not new to them. With harsh words and punishing hands, they forced the women to form a column. When a child wailed in terror or a woman cringed away from being touched, the men slapped them into orderly submission. No one was actually harmed, but Abigail saw the red marks spring up on slapped faces or twisted wrists. She turned, briefly, to Ahinoam.

"Keep Amnon quiet," she hissed. "Don't let him cry or struggle."

Ahinoam was white with fear. Her eyes rolled like a nervous colt's. "He minds you better than me," she whispered.

"But I have Chileab," Abigail began — then quickly, before her willingness subsided, "Here, give him to me. Put him in this arm, and I'll hold Chileab on the other side. Amnon, listen to me! If you cry, I'll whip you. Do you understand?"

The child nodded, but his lips trembled.

"Hold my neck tight," Abigail said. "Careful. Don't bump the baby with your feet. Show me what a big boy you can be."

I want to weep, she thought. *I want to shout curses at the vile man staring at me. And I'm reduced to saying the silly things one says to a frightened child.*

"Shall I take Chileab?" Topeleth asked softly behind Abigail. "I can carry him."

"No, you'll have all you can do to walk," Abigail said. "Is Rachel all right?"

A soldier brought his hand across Abigail's mouth in a stinging slap. "Shut up and walk," he shouted. "That goes for all of you. No talking or wailing. Just walk."

Abigail forced herself to stay calm, to meet Amnon's eyes with a smile. "Shh," she said. "Put your head on my shoulder. We're going for a walk."

Amazingly, Amnon dropped his head onto her shoulder, his fear revealed only in the spasmodic clutch of his arms around her neck. The weight of the two children made Abigail awkward, but she knew that other women were carrying two children — perhaps some were carrying two and leading a third. She could do as much.

The looters were spilling back into the street, piling jars and wool and trinkets onto the backs of the patient camels. With a wince of real pain, Abigail saw her lyre and David's carried from the house and strapped to a shaggy beast.

But all the time, her ability to accept things realistically kept her from grieving too much over the plundering and destruction. While some of the women moaned or cried out until they were slapped into silence, she could only be thankful that they were all alive, that, except for some slaps and bruises, no one had been hurt.

Suddenly, a woman cried out shrilly, and Abigail looked up to see the first tongues of flame lick against the sky. *If it were Hebron being put to the torch,* she thought, *the pain in my heart would be unbearable. But this town means nothing to me— to any of us. The small things that hold our memories are already strapped to the camels that are being led away.*

Still, there was a painful finality in seeing the fire take over the town. When David and his men came back to Ziklag, they would find only ashes and rubble where once their wives and children had waited.

"Don't stand and gawk!" A large hand jerked Abigail's arm and jolted her into action. "No amount of tears will put out the fire. Come on now, keep walking."

"I don't see any weeping," Abigail retorted. She moved swiftly along with the column of women before the soldier could strike her. She had seen one blow, intended for a woman, land on a baby, and she didn't want that to happen to the children in her arms. Without a look of farewell at Ziklag, she set her face toward the south and began to plod along the dusty track.

It seemed as though the day would never end. Weary, hot, thirsty, and frightened, the women and children stumbled after their captors. Several times during the afternoon they were offered water, and a few stops had been permitted — not really long enough for a baby to be fully fed. So by the time the raiders stopped to make camp, the women were barely able to stay on their feet.

When permission was granted, they dropped to the ground and huddled together, hoping only that Dorfu's orders would truly be carried out and that they would be unmolested for this night at least. Scant rations were handed out among them, and somehow the children were fed and pacified with promises that their mothers knew could not be kept.

Topeleth was a tower of strength to everyone. She was so soft-spoken and courteous to the captors that no one lifted a hand to her, and almost automatically, she became a sort of mediator. More and more, she was allowed to go from woman to woman, sharing what small scraps of comfort she could gather up.

"I heard the leader — the one they call Dorfu — talking to his men," she whispered to Abigail. "None of us will be molested or hurt. It might help if you — if you were not so insolent."

"I can't help it," Abigail said. "They chill my blood!"

"They have all the weapons and all the power."

"We still have Yahweh," Abigail said, her voice stubborn. "Surely He will save the sons of David."

"Then let David's wives be patient," Topeleth said, but gently.

"I'll try," Abigail answered faintly, "but if he comes near me — that Dorfu — if he comes near me, I'll — I'll spit."

"You'll behave properly," Topeleth said. "You would only endanger your son by indulging your own pride."

"Oh, I know, I know," Abigail said. She bent her head over the child at her breast.

A soldier suddenly appeared before them. "Our lord, Dorfu, wants to talk to you," he said roughly to Abigail.

"When I've finished feeding my son," she said.

The man, obviously frustrated and already angry, erupted in a torrent of anger and abuse. "You treat me with the respect you owe me," he shouted. "When I say our lord wants to talk to you, I mean *now*."

Abruptly, he leaned forward to snatch the baby out of Abigail's arms. He held Chileab by one small leg, and the baby cried shrilly in pain.

Abigail flew up from the ground. "Leave him alone," she screamed. "Get your filthy hands off him."

With a quick rage, the man suddenly swung the baby in a sort of wringing motion, and Abigail heard the fragile splintering of bone. The baby's shriek rose to an unbearable crescendo and then stopped so suddenly that Abigail felt her heart stop, too.

"You've killed him," she raved. "You've killed him."

She sprang on the man, clawing at his face. With a grunt, he tossed the baby to Topeleth and turned to vent his wrath on Abigail.

Dorfu's voice thundered between them. "What did I tell you? What have you done to the child?"

"He killed him," Abigail sobbed, trying vainly to free her hands from the bandit's imprisoning hold.

"I merely twisted his leg," the man panted. Abigail kicked him and heard his breath whistle out in pain and surprise.

"No," Topeleth cried. "He's not dead, Abigail. He's unconscious, but he's breathing. Truly, my dear. Come and get him. He needs you."

"Let her go," Dorfu barked. "Go to my tent. I'll tend to you later."

Abigail, released from the numbing hold, ran to Topeleth and took the baby into her arms. With wildly shaking hands, she pulled the covers away from the tiny body. One leg, grotesquely twisted and swollen, hung as though it did not belong to the rest of his body.

"Oh, Yahweh, my Lord," Abigail gasped.

"Is he dead?" Dorfu asked.

"He's terribly hurt," Topeleth answered.

"The man will be punished," Dorfu said. "Can you mend him, do you think?"

Abigail neither looked up nor answered. If the child lived, he would never walk normally. He was unfit to be the son of a king. Her heart, as twisted and maimed as the small leg, fluttered in her chest like a wounded butterfly.

"We'll try to mend him," Topeleth said calmly, in spite of the tears that rolled down her face. "I think his mother will not be able to talk to you tonight, my lord."

"Time enough," Dorfu said indifferently. "Mend the child if you can. If he dies, why, then, he dies."

He turned and left the women. Almost at once, the crack of a whip and the screams of a whipped man could be heard. When he was finally quiet, a silence fell over both the women and their captors.

In a cold, white fury, Abigail worked with her battered child. One of the women had brought a small bag of spices, and Rachel worked them into a poultice. They wrapped this about the tiny leg and bandaged it with strips of cloth which Abigail tore from her robe. Halfway through the procedure, Chileab began to cry — a small, hesitant whimper at first, like the cry of a hurt animal. But later, when Abigail had fed him a little, he screamed in anger and pain.

She drank in the sound as though it were music. As long as he had the strength to cry so lustily, she dared to hope, for hadn't David said that, even if the child were not perfect, he would still love him?

The women who had faced the destruction of their houses and the loss of everything they owned with calm, set faces, wept with the baby.

"I can't stand it," Ahinoam said. "What will our lord say? And I have no comfort to offer him. I have discovered only today that I have not conceived a child."

Rachel made no comment other than to offer her constant presence, her stricken face, and her tears. But Topeleth, who had mourned the children who had been too weak to live, knelt on the ground beside Abigail and kept whispering fiercely, "He'll live, my child. He will! No pagan dog can destroy the son of David."

21

TOWARD EVENING of the first day's journey, at the same hour that Dorfu and his men had halted with their captives, the troops of Achish and David made camp on the eastern plain. Mt. Gilboa was in sight but at least another day-and-a-half journey away. Because the Philistine troops issued no invitation to share their campsite, David and his men formed their own camp, built their own campfire, and erected their own small shelters against the night.

Darkness had hardly fallen when a messenger came to David.

"My lord Achish bids you come," he said.

David looked across the fire to catch the eyes of Joab. "I thought the son of Jesse was not welcome in the tent of our lord Achish," he said bitterly. "There has been no sign of friendship during this whole journey."

"Well, now you're invited," Joab said dryly.

"Do you need anyone to go with you?" Benjamin asked, his voice brittle with challenge.

David looked at the messenger. "The invitation is only for me, is it not?" he asked.

"Only for you, my lord," the messenger said in an expressionless voice.

David got up without saying anything more, and, still

silent, followed the messenger to the tent of Achish, where rich, embroidered draperies had been hung to shut out the night air.

"You sent for me, my lord?" David asked when he had entered the tent.

Achish's face was strained with worry. "My son, you know I trust you," he began. The lack of amenities only underlined the importance of his summons.

David's voice was noncommittal in spite of the sudden apprehensive thrust of his heart. "I hope so, my lord," he murmured.

"But mine is not the only voice in my army," Achish said. "I have just met with some of the captains — at their request. They're deeply disturbed about something."

"I hope that neither I nor my men have done anything to offend you, my lord."

Achish's answer was hurried. "No, of course not. I've never found fault with you. Ever since the first day you came to join forces with me, I've been more than satisfied with you. But my captains don't share my confidence, I'm sorry to say. They think you and your troops should be sent back to Ziklag."

Although a great pulse of hope began to hammer in him, David kept his voice steady. "I'm sorry, my lord. I had hoped only to fight beside my lord in the battle against his enemies."

"I know," Achish said. "And I would trust you implicitly. But I dare not risk angering my captains. You can see that."

David nodded solemnly. "Yes, my lord. I can see the difficulty for you."

"So then," Achish said, "when morning comes, when it is first light, will you take your men and return to Ziklag? Will you go in peace, my son, feeling no bitterness toward me?"

David felt the pain of his nails biting into his palms, but he gripped his hands all the harder, knowing that if he did not exert control over himself, he would be shouting and capering like a man gone mad.

"Indeed," David said earnestly, holding a tight rein on his voice lest it scale up into a hymn of joy. "Indeed, my lord, I feel no bitterness toward you. I understand your position. As a leader of men, I, too, know what compromises one is forced to make."

Achish looked fondly at the young man before him. "I hoped you would understand. I'll tell my captains that you will leave us at dawn. While you head back to Ziklag, we'll make our way toward Mt. Gilboa. When I return from battle, we'll meet again, my son."

"Of course, my lord. I'll go and tell my men. If you'll excuse me, my lord?"

Achish nodded benignly, and David backed hurriedly from the tent. Even in the open air, he held his movements to those of a dejected man, pushing down hard on the longing to dance for joy at the miracle Yahweh had brought about.

Only when he was safely at his own fireside did he even let his voice show his exultation, and then only to Joab, Benjamin, and a few others. Men, miraculously released from an obligation they had dreaded, could not be trusted to conceal their joy. Time enough, when morning came and David's army was on its way back to Ziklag, to tell of the mercies which had been granted them.

David, himself, did not try to go to sleep for a long time. He sat, staring at the starred sky, song fragments winding and unwinding themselves through his mind. Words of praise shaped and reshaped themselves.

"I will bless the Lord at all times;
His praise shall continually be in my mouth.
My soul shall make its boast in the Lord,
The humble shall hear it and rejoice.
O magnify the Lord with me,
And let us exult His name forever."

These words, or words like them, had been begging to be put to music for weeks, but David's heart had been too heavy. Now, out of his wild exultation, the words and music blended into perfect harmony in his mind.

"I sought the Lord, and He answered me,
And delivered me from all my fears...."
David sang silently and confidently to himself, "This
poor man cried and the Lord heard him,
And saved him out of all his troubles.
The angel of the Lord encamps around those who fear
    Him,
And rescues them."
Some of the men groaned or muttered in their sleep. "Let
them groan," David gloated, glancing around him. "In the
morning, I'll give them the most glorious news of their
lives. It will be the beginning of a day of joy."

He closed his eyes and tried to quiet his mind and heart.
In only a few hours, he thought, *I'll see Abigail again —
Abigail who was so sure this miracle would happen. Oh, Yahweh,
my Lord, my God, I will never doubt You again. Abigail was right.
You are to be trusted utterly.*

His mind was still elevated to heights of praise and joy the
following afternoon when he caught his first glimpse of
Ziklag in the distance. Lazy twists of pale smoke climbed
above the walls of the town, and even in the first minute,
David knew that this was not the smoke of cooking fires.

He pushed his mule to a hard gallop, and a number of
men, as alarmed as he, rode closely behind him.

At the ruined gate, with the stench of the charred city in
his nostrils, David stopped, stunned.

A cry of desolation and fear broke out among the men,
and they swept by David into the smoking rubble. They
found nothing, of course, except the bodies of the sentries.

"What are you going to do?" one of the men screamed at
David. "You claim Yahweh sent us back. Back to what?
What are you going to *do?*" He stooped to the ground,
grasped a chunk of stone, and stood again, his arm cocked as
though to throw.

David looked from man to man, seeing only anger, horror,
and rage in the eyes of the men who usually looked to him
with obedience and love.

"I don't know," David whispered. "I don't know." His chin sank to his chest, and shuddering sobs shook him as though he were a bit of grass blown by a winter wind.

When the Amalekites broke camp the next morning, Abigail noticed, in spite of her agony over Chileab, that a young Egyptian, sick and feverish, was being left heartlessly behind. She glanced with pity at the young man who lay helplessly in a field, far from water, and knew that this act of desertion symbolized the kind of people who had captured them. She could not hope for mercy or gentleness from men who would leave a comrade to die alone.

Chileab's whole body was hot to Abigail's touch, and every movement brought a shrill, pitiful cry from him. But miraculously, he continued to nurse, and she knew that as long as she could get nourishment into him, there was a chance that he would live.

During one dark hour of their second night on the trail, she wondered bleakly if it would be better simply to let the baby die. Perhaps if she didn't feed him or if they discarded the sling in which she and Rachel carried him to reduce jostling him, then he would die. Surely he would be killed anyhow when they reached their destination, and certainly the deed would not be done with mercy. These Amalekite pagans would have no use for a crippled boy.

But while these evil thoughts twisted through her tired mind, Topeleth came up to Abigail.

"Are you all right?" she whispered. "Here's a bit of cool water I saved. Can you use it to bathe his poor little face, to wet his lips?"

Abigail fumbled for the water, refreshed as though she had been drinking it herself. Sanity and hope and decency were in the tired old voice, and Abigail absorbed the sound of them into her heart.

"Aunt Topeleth," she whispered, "I love you. I've never told you. I'll be grateful all my life that I married Nabal — just because of you."

"Why, my dear." The old voice faltered and stopped. When she spoke again, it was obvious she had been moved to tears. "No one ever said that to me before. Not anyone. You've made me very, very happy."

In the midst of the desert night, with fear and cruelty all around them, Topeleth could speak of happiness. *Yahweh must have put her in my life*, Abigail reflected humbly, *to give me courage when I needed it most.*

"Let me sit beside him," Topeleth said. "You sleep for a little while. You'll need your strength for tomorrow."

Obediently, Abigail lay down, and then, miraculously, she slept.

As she slept, she dreamed that she was back again, safe and sheltered, on the rooftop in Hebron. Her father sat beside her, holding Chileab in his arms.

"Every son of David cannot be a king," Eliab said in a voice that sounded strangely like Samuel's. "If this child is lame, at least he will not plot against his father. Perhaps he'll sing David's songs and play the lyre and dream great dreams — the dreams of David."

His voice repeated the name over and over, and for the third time in her life, Abigail's dream swelled and soared with the sound of David's name. The sky shimmered and roared, and the whole earth shook with a thunderous affirmation.

She woke with a start, the dream etched vividly in her mind. She went back over it carefully, remembering every bit of it. She knew, now, that such dreams held prophecy in them. Surely this dream meant that Chileab would live and that David would defeat his enemies — even these Amalekites who had captured his wives and children.

Chileab was weak and listless in the morning but still able to nurse, still able to cry out in anger at his pain. Abigail and Rachel held the small sling between them and matched their steps as well as they could so the little body would not be jolted.

Just after noon, they came to a wide oasis which was obviously home to the captors. The women of Ziklag watched in silence as wild reunions took place before them. They listened to the shouts of joy and the greedy squeals of women who received the spoils of the raid.

One of the men finally herded Abigail and the others to a shaded spot on one side of the oasis, where he gave them bread and figs and pointed out a spring of fresh water.

"When Dorfu's ready," he said, "someone will come to get you. You won't need a guard." A derisive wave pointed out the unrelenting stretch of desert around them. "Just keep the children quiet — and clean yourselves up."

After he left, the women sat wearily, feeding their children, using the cool water to wipe small faces.

The hours dragged by. The sounds from the other section of the oasis indicated that a wild celebration was underway. Obviously, the men were eating and drinking and dancing, and the raucous laughter and music spilled through the air.

The wildness of the celebration must have kept even the sentries from being observant, because evidently no one among the Amalekites saw what Abigail suddenly saw. Across the desert, swift and silent, came a wave of mounted men, swords held at the ready. The setting sun struck the man on the lead mule, and Abigail saw his face clearly. It was David come to rescue them.

22

THE NIGHTMARE SOUNDS of killing and dying, the shrieks of agony and yells of fury, went on for hours. Abigail, like the other women, huddled on the ground, waiting for some indication of how the battle was going.

Finally, Benjamin rode over to the frightened, sickened women at the edge of the oasis. He took time only to determine that they were unharmed; then he turned to do battle again.

Rachel called him back. "Your nephew was hurt," she called out coldly. "Almost mortally. And deliberately, my lord. They wrung his leg as though they were killing a pigeon."

Benjamin paused only long enough to shout, "Stay down. We'll send a few men to protect you all." But the fury of his face as he wheeled his mule was shocking.

"You've turned him into a madman," Abigail said in alarm. "I didn't know — I hadn't realized you could be so bloodthirsty."

Rachel smiled with grim satisfaction. "Your suffering, my sister, will not go unavenged this time. Whether it's right or wrong, the man who hurt Chileab will die."

Abigail only crouched on the ground, ministering to her maimed child. She didn't feel any of the gratification of revenge. Chileab had been perfect, and now he was lame.

If Benjamin and David killed every Amalekite in the world, they could not make Chileab whole again.

The sounds and smells of the slaughter seemed to go on and on. True to his word, Benjamin sent soldiers from David's army to form a protective ring around the women. But the men would not stay. Their rage was too fierce to permit such inactivity. All through the night, they would go, one by one, to join the murderous fighting, sending other weary soldiers back to take their places. That way, all the women were permitted brief reunions with their husbands, all but Ahinoam and Abigail. They waited in vain for a glimpse of David, for the reassurance that he was alive.

Toward morning, Benjamin came for a short respite. He drank deeply of the water offered to him, ate a handful of figs, touched his sleeping daughter with a gentle finger, held Rachel briefly, and then came to look at Chileab.

"His leg is broken," Abigail said. "Some common soldier did it. Dorfu — the leader, that is — had him whipped. They didn't intend this to happen, I'm sure."

Benjamin cursed under his breath as he knelt by his small, feverish nephew.

"Intentional or not," he said, "they'll pay. And pay and pay. I told David. He's like a madman."

He started to stand again, but Abigail held him back. "How did he find us?" she asked. "How did he get away from Achish in the first place?"

"It was a miracle," Benjamin said quickly. "The Philistine captains told Achish that David and his men were not to be trusted, so Achish sent us back to Ziklag. We came with such joy and found —" His voice broke off. He took a deep breath and went on. "David and Abiathar used the ephod to ask Yahweh's guidance. Yahweh told David to pursue. So, we pursued," he finished quickly, and moved again to get up.

"But how did you find us?"

"Are you trying to keep me from killing the enemy, my sister?" Benjamin asked quietly.

"No, truly. But please rest a minute more. What do you think it's like for us to sit here in the dark and hear the screaming — and not know —" This time it was her voice which broke in a sob.

Benjamin sat back. "I'll sit for five minutes," he said. "No more. We don't need rest, because Yahweh has filled us with a power. As to how we found you, there was an Egyptian found lying in a field."

"He was left behind to die," Abigail broke in. "They just left him there — with nothing — not even water."

"Then you must be the lady who looked at him with pity," Benjamin observed. "He said there was kindness in her eyes. I think it was partly because of you that the man agreed to lead us here."

"And partly because David promised not to kill him if he helped?" Abigail asked.

"Partly," Benjamin admitted.

"Never mind. He brought you here. Will the killing never cease, Benjamin?"

"When the last Amalekite is dead — or has escaped." Benjamin stated grimly. "And now, let me go."

"Benjamin, is my lord all right?" The words were hurried, almost as though she were afraid to say them. "I've seen almost every other man except him. Is he safe?"

"He's safe. But he says he won't give himself the privilege of seeing you until the enemy is killed. Don't accuse him of personal revenge when he comes, Abigail. Yahweh told him to do this."

"I know. I had another dream. I know that Yahweh still loves David. I knew you'd come."

"Well, then," Benjamin said, "You know what I have to do, so let me go."

This time she was silent and let him go. Then, like the other women, she waited for the battle to end.

It was nearly sunset when David finally came to where his women waited. Heady with victory, regretting only the escape of the tag end of the Amalekites who had fled across the desert on camels, he had evidently washed as much of the blood from his hands and clothes as possible. In each hand he carried a few items of jewelry. The reddish light from the setting sun cast a ruddy glow across his face and hair so that he looked, coming toward them, as though he were an angel instead of a man.

He stopped in front of Ahinoam first. "Are you all right?" he asked, dropping a light kiss on her cheek, and placing one pile of jewelry in her hands. "Is Amnon all right?"

"We're fine, my lord." She was rosy with pleasure that he had spoken to her first. Amnon looked up from the dust he was scraping into piles and smiled radiantly at his father. David swung him high above his head, and for just a second the small, upside-down face was like a mirror held above David's uptilted face.

David placed the little boy close to Ahinoam. "Thank you for taking care of him," he said.

Abigail, hearing the words, winced in pain. It had never occurred to her that David might think *she* had failed Chileab. The tears she had held back during the last three days of agony began to build up like a stinging wall behind her eyes.

David stood in front of her. "I'm here, my love," he said.

No words could be forced past the aching lump in her throat, so she only looked at him in silence, feeling the first of the tears slipping down her cheeks.

"Are you sorry to see me back?" David asked in a voice so soft that no one else could hear.

"S-sorry?" she choked out. "Oh, my lord, my — my beloved."

David reached for her and, in sight of all, pulled her close to him and held her as though he could never let her go.

"The baby's hurt," she gasped, breathless in his hold. "It wasn't my fault, truly, truly, my lord. I —"

"Hush." His voice was so gentle that it seemed incredible that he had just come from the slaughter of men, women, and children. "I know what happened. A dozen men have told me what their women told them. I know how you went for the soldier like a spitting cat. I know, my love, I know."

"Oh, my lord, I've missed you so!"

For another long moment he held her, and then he loosened his arms. "Let me see him," he said softly. "Let me see what they did to my son."

He said nothing as he knelt in the dirt to examine Chileab. She saw how he clenched his jaw against anger or despair, and although he brushed them away at once, she saw the tears that glistened in his eyes.

"You said you'd love him," Abigail said. "Even if he weren't perfect, you said you'd love him."

"Did you have foreknowledge of this?"

"Oh, no, my lord. Just some — some premonition of my inability to have a son fit to succeed you."

David sat back on his heels. "There will be other sons," he murmured, almost absently. "The important thing is to keep him alive, to take care of him."

"Oh, yes, my lord." Her relief was so intense that she felt she could not bear it after so much pain.

"If Yahweh wants him to live, he *will* live," David said. He was different, she saw. Yahweh had come into his life in a more vital way than He ever had before.

"Now," David said. "It's time for me to rest. As soon as it's light, we'll start back. I wish I could lie beside you, for no other reason than to hear your breathing. But the men will stay apart from their women."

"Yes, my lord," she whispered. "I understand."

David's lips brushed hers, and then he turned to move away. "Oh, by the way," he said, looking back at her with a smile, "I even found the lyres and saved them both. We'll make music together yet, my love."

There was no sense of homecoming when David's people arrived back in Ziklag. The burned-out town offered no shelter or comfort, and the sense of being in a foreign country seemed to be a growing emotion in everyone.

The miracle to Abigail was that Chileab was still alive, that although he cried often from pain, he had survived the cruel trip back across the desert. On their arrival at Ziklag, the priest, Abiathar, had taken the small leg in his large hands and, with a motion too quick to be identified, pulled the leg into a more normal position. Chileab screamed in a voice that stabbed Abigail to the heart, but later, when the child had been soothed with nourishment and rest, it was obvious to everyone that the leg was not as deformed as it had been.

"He may never march into battle," Abiathar said to Abigail, "but I think he'll walk. Not perfectly. He probably won't —" He hesitated, groping for the kindest words.

"He'll never succeed his father as king," Abigail said. "I know that. It doesn't matter, my lord."

"May Yahweh bless the boy with other talents," the priest intoned. "May Yahweh give him health and peace."

From that moment on the baby improved, and before three days had gone by, Abigail knew that the danger was past.

David was busy with a dozen projects. He had sent some of the spoils taken from the Amalekites to all the villages of southern Judah. The men who carried the spoils also carried the message that David had not, indeed, gone to war against the Israelites. Yahweh had wrought a miracle, the messengers were to relate. Yahweh had filled the Philistine captains' hearts with resentment against David, so that Achish had been forced to send the young Hebrew and his men back to Ziklag.

"Can't you see what will happen?" David said to Abigail. "The villagers will be so grateful for the spoils, so happy with the account of Yahweh's goodness to me, that when the time comes, they'll be eager to have me come home."

"A clever move, my lord," Abigail said.

David looked sternly at her. "Not clever. Yahweh has shown me what to do."

"Yes, my lord." She felt a great sense of relief. Not so long ago, he had been smitten with his own cleverness. Now he

gave credit where it belonged. If David were to be a king of
Israel, he had to be a man who walked with his God.

"When do you think the time will come, my lord?" she
asked. "Do you think it will be soon?"

"I don't know," David admitted. "I seem to be waiting,
and I don't know what I'm waiting for."

They had, in fact, only a few hours to wait. Just before
sunset, a weary, dirty stranger came gasping to the gate of
Ziklag with the dark announcement that Saul and Jonathan
had both been killed in battle, and that their severed heads
had been hung on stakes above the walls of Beth-shan.

23

IN THE LONG, taut, drawn out silence following the dreadful announcement, David stood as though he had been turned to stone. Because the burned houses offered no decent refuge, the people were all gathered together in an open area of the town, so even the women heard the words.

In spite of the stricken look on David's face, Abigail's first reaction was a sweet, swelling sense of relief. If Saul were dead, then David need no longer hide in wilderness caves or in the towns of the uncircumcised. If Saul were dead, they could go home.

Then, as David's silence continued, she began to discern the grief which gripped him. It was the death of Jonathan, of course — Jonathan who had been David's dearest friend, Jonathan who had once risked his life and the love of his father for his constant companion, David.

David turned blindly toward the men who stood in silence behind him, and Abigail saw that his face was gray and stiff, as though with unutterable fatigue. In that instant she knew that he would not look so bereft if the news had been brought of her death.

David turned back to the messenger. "How do you know that Saul and Jonathan are dead?" he asked in a bleak voice.

"Because I saw Jonathan's body, my lord. With my own

eyes I saw it. And, as for King Saul, he had been mortally wounded, my lord, and begged me to kill him so that the Philistines would not torture him. I ran him through with his own sword, as he begged me to."

David swayed a little as though he might fall. "And who are you?" he asked in a voice that was bleached of all emotion.

"I'm an Amalekite, sir," the man said, "the son of an alien."

Does he expect David to reward him for his grisly news? Abigail thought. *Does he think David is so hungry for power that he would befriend the man who had killed the Lord's anointed? The man is a fool.*

David looked at Ethan, who stood near the messenger, and said, "Kill him. Strike him down for what he has done."

Ethan's knife flashed in the air, and the young messenger lay, still and bleeding, in the dust. It had happened so fast that Abigail could not feel any sensation of dismay.

David stood looking down at the fallen messenger. "Your blood is on your own head," he said in a hard voice. "You testified against yourself when you admitted you had killed the Lord's anointed."

With stiff, controlled movements, David turned from the dead body on the ground. Lifting his hands to the neck of his robe, he grasped both sides of the neck opening, and with a quick, strong gesture, he ripped the robe open almost to his waist. Looking neither left nor right, he walked until he was separated from the crowd of his followers and family. There he sat on the ground, gathered up handfuls of dust, and trickled them over his head and shoulders. Then he threw back his head and wept.

"How he mourns for Saul," the people whispered.

"How can he weep for a man who chased us into the wilderness, who forced us into a pagan land?"

"But he never hated Saul. He spared his life twice."

"Three times."

"Only a great man can mourn his enemy."

"A great man."

"A man worthy to be king."

So the whispers ran.

Abigail watched and listened for a few minutes and then went back to the area that had been made into a shelter for a few of the women and children. *No one*, she thought, *no one loves him as much as I do. No one's heart breaks over him as mine does. And yet, I'm the only one who understands. I'm the only one who truly knows that his grief is genuine, but not for Saul. If he weeps for Saul at all, it is only to impress the people. But the sorrow that turned his face gray is his sorrow over Jonathan.*

Well, then, that was part of the burden of love — to know the weaknesses and the sins of the beloved and to feel no lessening of loyalty.

She lifted her baby to her breast, and for the first time since he had been hurt, he didn't cry out at her touch. His small mouth, shaped like her father's mouth, turned up in a hesitant, wavering smile. *Life is a mystery*, Abigail's thoughts went on. *Yahweh gives us tragedy and loss, and then the small miracle of a baby's first smile — a baby who might never have smiled at all.*

David and his men fasted until sundown, and then gradually the men sought and found a place to sleep.

David continued to sit alone, silent and shrunken, his head between his hands. Abigail came to him on quiet feet, his lyre in her arms.

"My lord," she whispered. "Would it ease you to make a song about it all? Or is it too soon?"

David stared at her as though she were a stranger. "What kind of man am I?" he asked hoarsely, "that I sit here shaping a song when my friend is dead? And how did you know?"

"Because," she said, "the night Chileab was hurt — dying, I thought — a dark song ran over and over through my mind. If I had dared sing it, some of the sorrow might have been eased."

David took the lyre in his dusty hands. The song spilled

out in plaintive, minor chords, but it was perfectly obvious that the song had come, full-blown, into his mind. Sometimes Yahweh gave a singer such a gift—a song, perfect and complete. Abigail had known that for a long time.

"Your beauty, O Israel, is slain on your high places!" David sang in a sad, husky voice, and Abigail felt the flesh on her arms prickle at the haunting beauty.

"How have the mighty fallen!
Tell it not in Gath,
Proclaim it not in the streets of Ashkelon;
Lest the daughters of the Philistines rejoice,
Lest the daughters of the uncircumcised exult.
O mountains of Gilboa,
Let not dew or rain be on you, nor fields of offerings;
For there the shield of the mighty was defiled,
The shield of Saul, not anointed with oil.
From the blood of the slain, from the fat of the mighty,
The bow of Jonathan did not turn back,
And the sword of Saul did not return empty.
Saul and Jonathan, beloved and pleasant in their life,
And in their death they were not parted;
They were swifter than eagles,
They were stronger than lions.
O daughters of Israel, weep over Saul,
Who clothed you luxuriously in scarlet,
Who put ornaments of gold on your apparel.
How have the mighty fallen in the midst of the battle!
Jonathan is slain on your high places.
I am distressed for you, my brother Jonathan;
You have been very pleasant to me.
Your love to me was more wonderful
Than the love of women.
How have the mighty fallen,
And the weapons of war perished!"

His voice faded away, but Abigail felt her own tears falling across her cheeks. Saul hadn't clothed *her* with scarlet, she reflected. Instead, he had banished her to the wilderness. But to such a wilderness, she thought, remembering the cave at En Gedi. She owed much to Saul. If he had not sent David away, she would never have become David's wife.

"Come, my lord," she whispered, making no attempt to wipe away her tears, "come and lie down on your pallet in a corner. You can't grieve forever."

David looked up from the lyre. "The words of the song are true," he said in a ragged whisper. "In spite of everything, the words are sincere. You've got to believe that."

"I believe it, my lord. What's more, the people believe it. I heard them talking, my lord. They're ready to make you king."

David glanced at her quickly, and she saw, in the light of the fire, the quick flame of joy in his eyes, even though there was still a glint of tears on his lashes.

Benjamin had been among the men who had been sent to take the spoils of war to the villages of Judah. He had gone to Hebron with David's gift and David's message, and he got back to Ziklag before noon the next day.

David and Joab were closeted in a room not ruined by the fire, so Benjamin came first to Abigail.

"Does he know about Saul?" Benjamin asked, not even bothering to identify David by name. "Does he know what happened to Jonathan?"

"How do *you* know?" she countered.

"The news has spread faster than a brush fire spreads. All over Judah, people are lamenting or rejoicing, depending on their feeling. The men of the village of Jabesh-gilead walked all night to take down the heads of Jonathan and Saul from the walls of Beth-shan — and their bodies — and buried them decently and with reverence. Their bones are buried under a tamarisk tree, and even now, the people are fasting for Saul."

She listened to his account with a sense of foreboding.

"Do you mean that the people are grieving so much for Saul that they won't even want my lord to come home?"

Benjamin's eyes shone. "No, not that at all. They grieve that Saul and Jonathan were killed by the Philistine dogs." He glanced around quickly to see if he could be overheard. "But they're tired of the problems of Saul's madness; they want a new king who can give them sanity and power."

"A man like my lord David."

"I heard his name everywhere I went," Benjamin admitted. "It was as though the whole earth were speaking of David."

"I know." This was what her dreams had foretold, that all the earth would say the name of David. "I think you ought to go and tell him. He's there, behind that wall, with Joab."

Benjamin nodded, but before he turned away he said, "Our parents sent their love and their sorrow about Chileab. They're eager for us all to come home. If David's willing, I think we ought to go back to Hebron. At once. Maybe even start this afternoon."

"Do you think he'll really be welcome in Hebron?" she asked.

"It will be in Hebron," Benjamin predicted, "that David will be made king of Judah. I'm sure of it."

He left her then, and she turned to find Ahinoam watching her.

"You heard?" Abigail said.

"Yes, I couldn't help it. I didn't mean to intrude."

"Don't be silly," Abigail said. "You have a right to know as much as I — or more."

Ahinoam smiled. "I'm glad we'll go to Hebron. I might have thought once that to have him made king in my own city would have been fine. But, well, I'm glad it will be *your* town."

"Because Amnon is perfect and Chileab isn't?" Abigail asked gently.

Ahinoam nodded with a shamed look. "I feel so guilty that my own son is whole, while yours —"

Abigail stood looking at the kind, sweet face with its worried look. Ahinoam was like a child, riddled with small greeds and large generosities. *And if David ever takes another wife to heart as well as to his bed,* Abigail thought, *this girl will be my comfort, whether I have earned her love or not.*

Impulsively, Abigail leaned forward and kissed Ahinoam's cheek. "Thank you, my sister," she said. "You're better to me than you should be."

Ahinoam shook her head. "Oh, no," she began, but a call interrupted them. David was striding toward them, his face blazing with excitement. "Abigail," he shouted, "we're going to Hebron. Benjamin says the time is right. Do you think Chileab can stand the journey?"

"Oh, yes, my lord," she said, breathless at the enormity of what was happening.

David didn't even glance at Ahinoam. He grabbed Abigail and swung her in an exuberant circle. "You know what this means?" he exulted. "You do know?"

It was as though his grief had never been.

"Oh, yes, my lord." Her voice bubbled with sudden laughter. She had thought, huddled over Chileab in the desert, that she would never laugh again.

"Then hurry," David said, giving her a little shake. "We'll start before Achish can possibly get back to Philistia. We'll shake the dust of this ruined city from our feet — and we'll never really rest until we're home."

He released Abigail, brushed a gentle hand across her hair, and swung to rejoin the men. It was only then that he saw Ahinoam.

"Well, mother of Amnon," he said gaily. "Will you, too, be glad to return to Judah?"

"I would go anywhere my lord wishes," Ahinoam said in her light, colorless voice.

But David's exuberance was too brilliant to be dimmed by anyone. "Then hurry and help Abigail," he said. "We're going home." He started away and then turned once more to Abigail. "Do you think your father would let us sleep in his house?" he said softly. "Until our own house is ready, do you think he would?" His eyes were bright.

Her voice was steady, but her heart was thundering in her ears. "My father would do anything that would serve the king of Judah, my lord."

She was rewarded with an intensified flame in David's eyes more golden than the sun.

24

"DO YOU PLAN to make a shepherd out of the little one, that you bring him out here in the fields?" Eliab's question was genial, his voice betraying none of the grief that Abigail knew had been his ever since the day they had arrived in Hebron and Eliab had seen his grandson's twisted leg.

"Why not?" she answered, smiling. "He could do worse than be a shepherd."

"The son of a king?"

"But unfit to be a true prince," Abigail countered, "and besides, his father is not yet king."

"He would be, if the men of Judah had the decision to make," Eliab insisted. "It's his own modesty that holds him back."

"Not modesty, Father. Shrewdness."

"I can't believe you'd be critical of him, my child. I would have guessed that he possessed all of your heart."

"I don't love him blindly, Father. I understand him very well."

Eliab chuckled. "Yes, well, all right, shrewdness, if you will. But — shrewdness or modesty — it's his own decision to postpone his being made king. How long will he wait, do you think?"

"I don't know," she answered, her voice suddenly bitter. "He doesn't seem to have time to talk to me anymore."

"David's too busy now to think of you or confide in you.

He has other thoughts on his mind. Can't you accept that?"

"Whether I can accept it or not," she answered with no change of tone, "I'll have to get used to it, I guess. When there are battles — or consultations with other kings — or when he takes other wives, then I suppose I'll no longer matter to him."

"You disappoint me," he said. "It was your own decision to marry David. You *knew* he would be king. Did you expect to keep him dangling from a woman's fingers?"

She stared at him, shocked by his bluntness. "I'm sorry I'm such a disappointment to you."

Eliab smiled grimly. "If you said that with humility instead of ill humor, I'd be better pleased."

"I'm lonely," Abigail cried out, stung. "Rachel has Benjamin, and Ahinoam and my mother talk about — about nothing. And David — David goes his own way."

"He comes to you at night," Eliab said.

"He used to come to me for more than love," Abigail whispered. "We used to talk."

A touch of pity softened Eliab's mouth. "And he may again," he said. "When things are settled, when the men are all housed, when his plans are made —"

"Oh, I know, I know," she interrupted. "It's just —" She stopped, unable to justify her feelings. Her eyes fell. "I'm sorry," she mumbled.

Eliab's face softened even more. "And I'm sorry, too," he said. "I've been too hard on you. But I'm right, Abigail. You have to let him go. Well — give the baby to me. Let me take him over where the lambs are with their mothers."

She put the baby in her father's arms. "Won't he be a bother?"

Eliab's voice was gentle. "I took both you and Benjamin out to see the lambs before you were old enough to sit alone. It's a foolish whim of mine — that a child should see something as helpless and young as he is."

She tried to smile. "That's why I brought Chileab out here — because I remember how I loved it when I was little."

"And I scolded you," Eliab said. "But you see, my child, I

want you to be as perfect as Yahweh intended you to be."

She only nodded and then watched as Eliab moved across the field to where the lambs were nuzzling their mothers. She saw him pick a shady spot to sit down, and very faintly she could hear the sound of his voice as he talked to his grandson.

He's a good man, Abigail thought. *He was only trying to help me, and I had no right to get sulky or angry. Why do I always want more than I have? Why can't I be like other women?*

She leaned back on her elbow, and her mind went sliding back down the years, touching the many days she had spent in the fields with her father. Surely there must have been rain sometimes, or her father must have been cross, but all she could remember was happiness.

"Oh, Yahweh," she prayed suddenly, "give me the wisdom my father wants for me. Give me the sort of wisdom that will help David." She shut her eyes against the dazzle of the sky so that she might concentrate on her prayer.

"Where's Chileab?" The voice was David's, and she looked up in amazement, wondering if her prayer had simply conjured the man out of the air.

"My lord!" she gasped. "You startled me. He's there — see — with my father."

"Your father must have seen me coming," David said, sitting down beside her. "Do you suppose he took the child to give us a minute or two to talk?"

"My father is very kind," she said. "He knows that I rarely have a chance to see you."

"Oh, come. I haven't been with Ahinoam once since we came to Hebron. I see you as much as your father sees your mother."

She tried to smile. "Forgive me, my lord. I'm being greedy — remembering how you talked to me during the days in En Gedi."

Without answering, David reached out and took her hand. For a short while, they sat in silence, hands clasped. It was almost like the way she used to sit with her father.

Abruptly, without warning, she was filled with the

memory of the day she had run to Eliab with some childish grief, and he had sat beside her, comforting her with a new and exciting story of Yahweh's holy Ark.

She remembered vividly how she had reacted to the story — her childish anger at the Philistines who had stolen the Ark, her glee over the bad luck that had befallen the captors until the Ark had finally been taken back again by Israelites. She remembered that the story had ended with the revelation that the Ark had been taken to the small town of Kirjath-jearim and had been placed there in hiding, waiting for the day when the sons of Yahweh would have the courage to claim it again for public display as the dwelling place of the Most High God.

David interrupted her thoughts. "I haven't been able to talk to you as I used to," he said, "because I'm still grieved over Jonathan — but it's more than that. I'm worried about whether or not I can bring the tribes of Judah, and eventually Israel, together. I'm not sure, in fact, that I'm fit to be king." There was despair in his voice.

She sat closer to him, forgetting herself in the face of David's need. "My lord," she said breathlessly. "You *are* fit to be king. Don't ever doubt it. And there *is* a way to bring the people together. I've just thought of it."

David looked at her with his eyebrows raised, and she felt her face flushing. "Not that I'm wiser than you, my lord," she said hastily. "But as I sat here, Yahweh put a memory in my mind. Remember the Ark of the Lord? Remember how it's been kept at Kirjath-jearim? What if, after you're king, my lord, you should go and bring the Ark to — to wherever it is that you'll rule? What if the people had the Ark as a symbol in front of them all the time — a sign that they were really Yahweh's people? That would bind them together, my lord. Better than any army, I think."

David sat in total stillness for a long time. "Of course," he said at last. "That's it. There's nothing else that could bind the people together like that. It will take a while, of course. I'll get Judah united, and then, when I think things are

right, I'll move up into Israel. And I'll bring the Ark home—
with singing and dancing and praise to Yahweh."

She gazed at him with delight, and David returned her
look without smiling.

"It's you," he said in a tone of discovery. "Ever since the
day you brought me food from Nabal's house, it has been
your wisdom and faith that have helped me. When I had to
go with Achish, when I came back to find Ziklag in ashes, it
was the memory of *your* faith and prayer that gave me
courage. Without you, I would have been lost."

"Truly, my lord?" Her voice was tremulous.

"Truly. I will thank my God for you as long as I live."

She was undone by his unexpected humility. That he
should say these things to her was beyond her dreams. And
if they were really true —

"Then — then there *was* a reason for Yahweh to bring me
to you?"

He made an impatient sound. "Can you ever doubt it?"
He was silent for a moment, then spoke with intensity.
"And do you honestly believe I am ready to be king?"

"Yes, my lord. Only *you* must believe it, too. Believe it
with all your heart."

"You'll never cease to pray for me? Even if I can't talk to
you as I used to? Even if — as king — I must walk alone?"

"I'll never stop praying, my lord," she promised. "But
you'll never have to walk alone. Yahweh will be your comfort and your guide. And I, my lord," she dared to say at
last, "I will love you until I die."

They were so absorbed in each other that they were
unaware of Eliab's approach until he spoke to them.

"The child is asleep," he said. "See — I have been as good
as a nursemaid."

David spoke casually, as though he were continuing an
interrupted conversation. "When he cries then, we'll know
where to turn, won't we, my love. Oh, and listen, my father,
will you tell the men of Judah that I'm ready now — I'm
ready to be their king?"

25

THE TOWN OF HEBRON bulged with men who had come from all over Judah to proclaim David king. On the high place, where an altar had been built for Samuel many years before, a floor had been constructed with an altar for sacrifice and a carved chair for the new king. All the women in town had used their precious store of spices to make sweet cakes, and whole sheep roasted slowly over fires which were carefully watched by boys. Every street bristled with the noise and bustle of celebration.

In Eliab's house, the confusion was only intensified. Both Zopporah and Eliab, conscious of their elevated position in the village because David was their son-in-law, ran from task to task, exhorting servants, scolding anyone who got in their way.

Abigail helped, following her mother's orders as though she were a child again. *No, not as though I were a child,* Abigail thought honestly. *As a child, I would have rebelled, wanting to be out in the fields with my father. I've actually improved a little.*

"Abigail!" David's voice came down from the upstairs room they had shared since arriving in Hebron. "Come here."

She ran up the steps, arriving breathless at the door of the room. "My lord," she said. "I thought you were outside with the men."

"Ought I to wear the apparel of a soldier or a shepherd or a king?" He stood in the middle of the floor, a simple white tunic draped over one arm, his sword clutched in the other hand.

She risked a smile. "What are you, my lord? Surely not a shepherd. To pretend to such humility might seem false. You've been a soldier for years, and today you'll be a king. I really don't know how to advise you."

"Of course you do." His voice was as petulant as a child's. "Come on now. What?"

She regarded him carefully. The people of Judah and Israel had only had one king, so there was really not much precedent for this day.

"Samuel had a lot to do with Saul's becoming king," she said slowly. "Have you made arrangements for Abiathar to conduct the ceremony?"

"Of course. Hadn't I told you that?" He sounded angry.

For a second Abigail felt the old pain, and then an unexpected gentleness filled her. Because she knew him so well, she saw the nervousness under the anger. David was frightened. He who could face giants and wolves, hordes of enemies or councils of unscrupulous men with courage, stood before her like a small boy.

"Well, then, let me think," she said. "The people will want a king, and in their minds a king is a soldier. So you should wear some sign of a soldier — a sword in your hand perhaps, or a heavy skin vest like the ones you wear for protection in battle."

She continued to examine him. "But there should be some sign of peace, perhaps even your lyre leaning against one side of your chair."

"Correct, and the sword will lean against the other side of the chair," David decided. "Benjamin is coming to escort me. Remind him to bring them."

"Yes, my lord." Her hands were busy, pulling the vest into place, smoothing the folds of the tunic. "There!" she said at last, stepping back. "I think you look just right."

"Fine." David started abruptly toward the door, then turned back to her. "I won't see you again until late. But no matter how late I am, wait for me. Tell your father we'll sleep on the roof tonight. Make sure my lyre is carried up there before dark."

"Yes, my lord."

He reached out and drew her close to him. "You are still so beautiful," he murmured. "How can you be so wise and yet so lovely?"

She smiled, too close to tears to risk speaking. He held her briefly, then turned on his heel to leave.

"Don't forget the lyre," he said over his shoulder. He was gone.

Abigail and Ahinoam had both been pushed into the front line of women who formed the outside circle around the place of honor. A small prominence of rock provided a vantage point for them so that they could see the ceremony taking place beside the altar. There was much pageantry in the offering of the sacrifice and in Abiathar's act of blessing as he poured the oil over David's head. Small golden beads of the perfumed oil caught the light of the sun and shone like jewels on David's bright hair and beard.

The people were silent during this part of the ceremony, and David's face was suffused with a radiance which Abigail had never seen before.

Abiathar took his hands from David's head. "Well, he's king at last," Ahinoam whispered. "Whether I wanted it or not, he's king at last."

Abigail nodded. "It wasn't what we wanted that mattered. It was what Yahweh wanted."

"And David," Ahinoam added.

"And David," Abigail agreed.

David turned to face the people thronged around him. His face was brighter than the sun's light that haloed his hair. "My people," he began. Immediately he changed the words. "People of Yahweh," he cried, "you have chosen me to lead you, but I come to you as a servant and a defender."

The people shouted out with a frenzy of approval, but Abigail, tearing her eyes away from David to look through the crowd, saw here and there a look of uncertainty, an expression of unfriendliness. She knew there were still followers of Saul in Judah. She prayed that Yahweh would give David the wisdom to know this and to win them to his side.

Benjamin, who stood close to David, leaned over and whispered in his ear. David nodded and quickly scanned the faces of the assembled men.

"My brother, Benjamin, has just told me something I hadn't clearly understood before," David announced. "He tells me that it was the men of Jabesh-gilead who buried Saul."

There was a sudden, complete hush. With unerring perception, Abigail picked out the delegation from Jabesh-gilead. The men seemed to gather together, obviously uncertain whether they were to be commended or censured for their act.

David left the platform, putting himself on a level with his people, and he, too, walked unhesitatingly to the men from Jabesh-gilead.

David paused in front of them and then spoke in a clear, carrying voice. "May you be blessed of the Lord because you have shown this kindness to Saul your lord, and have buried him."

No mention of Jonathan, Abigail noticed. How wise of David to speak only of the old, mad king who had hunted them through the wilderness. What better way for David to show his compassion and his loyalty to Saul's tribe of Kish?

"And now, may the Lord show lovingkindness and truth to you, and I also will show this goodness to you, because you have done this thing."

The men relaxed and stood with pride and confidence before David.

Sure of himself at last, all of his nervousness gone, David

smiled at them with a look of assurance. In ringing tones he concluded. "Now, therefore, let your hands be strong, and be valiant; for Saul your lord is dead, and the house of Judah has anointed me king over them."

How deftly he assumed the cloak of royalty, Abigail mused, *without destroying old loyalties to Saul. Surely this man has been guided by Yahweh.*

She looked around her and saw that the women, like the men, were gazing at David with adoration. There wasn't one of them who would ever deny his right to rule them.

David turned now toward the people in general. "Come," he cried out, "join me in the celebration — that Yahweh has given us another chance to be His people and do His will."

He was laughing, and the people laughed with him. Surrounding him, the men started down from the hill, ready for the victory feast. The women hurried to get ahead of them in order to serve them, so there was no chance for David to even look at the women of his household. His attention was completely captured by the men of Judah who had acclaimed him king.

The feasting lasted until long after dark. Abigail, like the other women, worked tirelessly to carry food and drink to the laughing, shouting men. Once during the evening, Abigail insisted that Topeleth, Rachel, Ahinoam, and Zopporah join her for a few minutes of rest and refreshment.

"As the women of the household of the king," she said, smiling, "surely we deserve a little rest, a bit of food."

"I'm only a sister-in-law," Rachel protested, but she sank onto the ground with a sigh of relief.

"And I only a mother-in-law," Zopporah added.

Topeleth smiled. "My claim is smallest of all," she said.

"But you're all beloved to me, and to Ahinoam," Abigail argued. "We five have shared so much. I want all of you to know how grateful I am."

She reached out her hands to them and felt the love with which they responded to her touch.

This is right, Abigail thought. *My duty now lies in rearing my son, in cherishing my mother and aunt, in loving my sisters. It won't be as exciting as sharing in the making of a king, but it is what I am supposed to do. I can only trust Yahweh to give me the grace to do it well.*

It was very late when David came wearily to the roof where Abigail waited.

"Are you here?" he asked, stopping at the top step.

"Here, my lord. I'm sorry there is no light. I let the lamp go out while I was admiring the stars. I'll take it down and light it."

"No, don't light it. Let me look at the stars, too."

Her eyes were adjusted to the dark, so she moved over to David and took his hand to lead him to a rug which she had spread in a corner.

"Here, my lord," she said. "Sit and rest. I know how tired you must be."

"Tired, yes," David admitted. "But I don't feel as though I can ever sleep. I've never felt so alive."

"It's not every day a man becomes a king," she said.

"No, it isn't," he agreed. "Oh, Abigail, Abigail, how I've longed for this day. How I've worked for it, dreamed of it."

"I know, my lord. Yahweh, Himself, has longed for it, I think."

David stared at her. "It's always you who brings me back to Yahweh. Don't fail to keep reminding me. I get so filled with admiration for my own cleverness that I sometimes forget the source of all wisdom."

"Just look at the stars, my lord. They'll remind you."

David lay back on the rug, pillowing his head on his arms. "I remember," he began quietly, "a night before I met you, a night in the desert when the stars blazed as they're burning now. I started a song — I've never finished it."

"How did it go, my lord?"

David hummed a fragment of tune, discarded it, and tried another. Finally he sang out with confidence.

"The heavens are telling of the glory of God;

And their expanse is declaring the work of His hands.
Day to day pours forth speech,
And night to night reveals knowledge."

Abigail listened in wonder; then she placed David's lyre
where his hands could reach it. He sat up, took the lyre, and
touched it with the assurance that comes only from inspira-
tion. The music and words poured out without faltering or
hesitation.

As he sang, Abigail's throat ached with a strange mixture
of pain and joy. There was pain in the knowledge that
David's kingship would take him away from her, but there
was joy in the certainty that she had helped him achieve his
destiny — and in so doing, had fulfilled her own.

As the song wove its spell around them, she was grateful
that he was sharing it with her. Not with Ahinoam or Joab
or the men of Judah, but with her — Abigail.

"Oh, Yahweh," she prayed with humility and love, "help
me always to remember that I have been given more than
most women ever have. Fill me with gratitude, not greed."

The long song wound down to a prayerful finish.

"Let the words of my mouth and the meditation of
    my heart
Be acceptable in Thy sight,
O Lord, my rock and my Redeemer."

The final chord hummed into silence, and David sat
immobile.

"My lord," Abigail said humbly, honestly, "you don't
need *me* to remind you that Yahweh rules your life. You
know a greater truth than I can ever know."

"Only when I open my heart to Him," David admitted.
"Sometimes I am blind and stubborn."

"But sometimes you are marvelous and wise," she said.

"Then may Yahweh make me wise more often than
foolish," David whispered with reverence. He lay down
quietly and put out his hand to her. "Will you lie beside me
without talking, without love? Will you be content to look at
the stars and think on the glory of our God?"

"Yes, my lord," she said.

They lay, not touching, both of them caught up in the holiness of the night. David finally slept, but Abigail was still awake when dawn lightened the eastern edge of the sky. Parts of David's song ran through her mind again and again. Even though she had heard it only once, some of the words were etched in her memory.

"Let the words of my mouth and the meditation of my heart," she whispered, watching the coming of day, "be acceptable in Thy sight, O Lord, my rock and my Redeemer."

The beauty of David's words, she thought with conviction, *will comfort me as long as I live — just as they will comfort all men who call on Yahweh as their God.*

CHRISTIAN HERALD ASSOCIATION AND ITS MINISTRIES

CHRISTIAN HERALD ASSOCIATION, founded in 1878, publishes The Christian Herald Magazine, one of the leading interdenominational religious monthlies in America. Through its wide circulation, it brings inspiring articles and the latest news of religious developments to many families. From the magazine's pages came the initiative for CHRISTIAN HERALD CHILDREN'S HOME and THE BOWERY MISSION, two individually supported not-for-profit corporations.

CHRISTIAN HERALD CHILDREN'S HOME, established in 1894, is the name for a unique and dynamic ministry to disadvantaged children, offering hope and opportunities which would not otherwise be available for reasons of poverty and neglect. The goal is to develop each child's potential and to demonstrate Christian compassion and understanding to children in need.

Mont Lawn is a permanent camp located in Bushkill, Pennsylvania. It is the focal point of a ministry which provides a healthful "vacation with a purpose" to children who without it would be confined to the streets of the city. Up to 1000 children between the ages of 7 and 11 come to Mont Lawn each year.

Christian Herald Children's Home maintains year-round contact with children by means of an *In-City Youth Ministry.* Central to its philosophy is the belief that only through sustained relationships and demonstrated concern can individual lives be truly enriched. Special emphasis is on individual guidance, spiritual and family counseling and tutoring. This follow-up ministry to inner-city children culminates for many in financial assistance toward higher education and career counseling.

THE BOWERY MISSION, located at 227 Bowery, New York City, has since 1879 been reaching out to the lost men on the Bowery, offering them what could be their last chance to rebuild their lives. Every man is fed, clothed and ministered to. Countless numbers have entered the 90-day residential rehabilitation program at the Bowery Mission. A concentrated ministry of counseling, medical care, nutrition therapy, Bible study and Gospel services awakens a man to spiritual renewal within himself.

These ministries are supported solely by the voluntary contributions of individuals and by legacies and bequests. Contributions are tax deductible. Checks should be made out either to CHRISTIAN HERALD CHILDREN'S HOME or to THE BOWERY MISSION.

Administrative Office: 40 Overlook Drive, Chappaqua, New York 10514
Telephone: (914) 769-9000